AN ISLAND LIFE

Chris Boult

Published by New Generation Publishing in 2019

Copyright © Chris Boult 2019

First Edition

The author asserts the moral right under the Copyright, Designs and Patents Act 1988 to be identified as the author of this work.

All Rights reserved. No part of this publication may be reproduced, stored in a retrieval system or transmitted, in any form or by any means without the prior consent of the author, nor be otherwise circulated in any form of binding or cover other than that which it is published and without a similar condition being imposed on the subsequent purchaser.

The original painting by John Connolly of 'Hawk Island' specifically commissioned for the book
www.connollyart.com

ISBN: 978-1-78955-711-4

www.newgeneration-publishing.com

New Generation Publishing

Previous titles

In The Shadow of the Bayonet
Out of the Shadow
Recovery
Green Terror
Identity
The Welsh Boys

About the Author

Chris studied in Nottingham in the late 1970s. He joined the OTC and the TA and later served as a short service officer in the regular army before joining the probation service in 1986. He served as a probation officer and a manager in various setting and at different levels, working mostly with high risk offenders and often closely with both the police and the prison service. He retired from service in 2015. He started writing novels in 2013 and this is his seventh book and the concluding part of the Emma and Rory trilogy.

Website: www.chrisboultauthor.co.uk

Chris is available to give talks to local groups on his experience of writing his own books.

Acknowledgements

Thanks to all involved in this process. A particular thanks to: my wife and my sister again for help in proofreading, my publisher and Titanic Brewery for their assistance. Also thanks to Sheila King of Chapters bookshop in Stafford, Sam Littlemore of The Words Worth bookshop in Eccleshall for their support for local authors and to all other venues that sell the books. Thanks to Lin Philips for her energy in organising local events for authors to share their work. Thanks to Martin Nolan and Dave Clough for their advice on Emma's business activities.

Thanks to all the lovely people at the Tyn-Y-Coed Hotel, the Moel Siabod Café and the many kind people we have encountered on Anglesey. All provided excellent hospitality over many years whilst visiting North Wales, including during the research undertaken for this book.

Thanks also to retired colleagues and those still working in criminal justice for their help with accuracy and to keep up to date with developments at work.

Acknowledgement too is due to Ryan who continues to help and advise me on photography and to my cousin, Jan, for advice on welsh language issues. Finally to John Connolly, who kindly lent his time and expertise as an artist to paint and create the front cover.

Author's note

This book is the third in a trilogy. It continues to tell the story of Emma and Rory's lives, interweaved with events concerning the Howell family. That is Bronwen and Glyn and her three sons, Ellis, Afan and Rhys.

It is based in mid-Staffordshire and North Wales, following on from the tragic death of David on the mountainside, with events running between June 2017 and May 2020. Again, whilst many of the places are real, I have continued to indulge in some poetic licence, with some places being entirely fictional, including the islands off the coast of Anglesey, which are the focus of the story. All the characters too are, of course, fictional.

The story is an attempt to speak to our aspirations for a better and more meaningful life, with stronger relationships and a greater sense of community. The potential is there if you can make it happen.

To all the innovators, explorers, risk-takers and philosophers in the pursuit of aspiration and contentment.

Glossary of terms

Supervision – The probation term for a regular meeting with your manager to discuss your performance and progress. Traditionally these meetings were also intended to offer personal support in recognition of the emotional and challenging dimensions of the job. Over time the emphasis has shifted more towards accountability with less focus on personal support.

CPS – Crown Prosecution Service.

Secondment – Deployment of probation staff to work in prisons for both the public and private prison sector.

Joint enterprise – The law relating to culpability in serious offences whereby a group rather than an individual can be convicted of, for example, murder.

Snouts – Informal term for police informants.

Tariff – The minimum term a life sentence prisoner must serve before consideration for release.

Category D – Open prison where prisoners are deemed to be 'low risk' and ready to start reintegration back into the community.

SOTP – Sex Offender Treatment Programme; the standard treatment approach for many years that has now been replaced.

Sentence Planning – the process in the prisons of matching risk and need to intervention.

SAS – Special Air Service – the elite of the elite of the army.

SBS – Special Boat Service – a similar elite of the navy.

REME – Royal Electrical and Mechanical Engineers – the army's AA, Halfords and more.

R and R – Rest and Recuperation.

PART ONE

Chapter One

June 2017

'Come on in, Poppy. Come and see your new house!' remarked Rory with all the joy, excitement and pride of a new father as he carried his daughter over the doorstep and into The Old School House for the first time.

Emma followed a little more carefully after the rigours of giving birth, but she was pleased and relieved that things had gone relatively well and that she had delivered a healthy child.

Poppy seemed somewhat underwhelmed as Rory swung her gently around the house in her car seat, explaining the intricacies of the building work that he and her mum had completed. By the time he had finished, she was comfortably asleep and they were free to put the kettle on.

'Well, Em, we've made it! Well done,' said Rory lovingly.

'This is only the start you realise, Rory Scott!'

'Yes and I'm loving it!'

'I've noticed.'

'You sit down, love, and I will fetch you a cup of tea.'

***

Over the following days, a succession of visitors called to see the baby and to see the family in their new home. As Emma had predicted, there was an air of excitement across the village, although Emma still feared the risk of intrusion from some people. She tried to keep calm and be tolerant, laugh it off and to recognise the joy in people's faces.

The vicar came, most of the neighbours and half the regulars from The Stag Inn. Copious invitations were issued to Poppy to tour the village and to be on show in the pub at the earliest opportunity.

Rory just lapped up all the attention and seemed to serve tea all day, whilst Emma was feeling tired and wished that the parade would come to an end. Breastfeeding at least offered the chance to disappear to the bedroom away from the visitors for a while. After some initial attempts to get the technique right, Poppy was feeding well on her mother's breast.

Emma had taken to motherhood better than she had expected. The whole pregnancy and birth had gone well, everyone kept telling her, and contrary to expectations she wasn't feeling too exhausted. Poppy showed early signs of being a good baby. She seemed quite content and was alert and responsive. Adjusting to limited and disturbed sleep was inevitably a challenge, but Emma found that she could respond, feed her and get back to sleep most of the time. She was pleased with her transition to being a mum and felt happy and proud to be so.

Emma reflected that she didn't even miss her corporate world, not yet anyway. The creation of her own business, although in its early stages, still seemed manageable and Rory had been very supportive. Emma never would have thought that she would reach a point in her life when her corporate business career seemed so unimportant to her. She'd done all that. She had established herself as a successful operator in the highly competitive world of business and finance and didn't feel that she had anything else left to prove to anyone, not least herself.

She had risen to the top in a male-dominated world, learnt to deal with the sexism, the put downs and the unwanted and uninvited attentions of men who regarded female attention as something of an entitlement. Once she had put down a marker and made it clear what she would or would not tolerate, her male colleagues generally seemed to respect her and managed to behave, for the most part, in a reasonable fashion.

Emma was personable, liked to socialise and liked male company. A certain level of flirting could be fun but a dinner date was not an agreement to anything else. Emma was aware of male gossip in the office and avoided overfamiliarity and the intrusion inherent in the overuse of social media.

Her corporate life seemed a long time ago already and carving out an independent career now seemed much more appealing, and much more compatible with this new chapter of her family life.

Life in The Old School House in Coppermere was inevitably overtaken and dominated by the arrival of one Miss Poppy May Scott. Her apparel lay strewn across seemingly all the rooms of the house. The paraphernalia of babies and young children – the cot, the bouncy chair, the feeding ancillaries, the flexible car seat, the push chair and of course the extensive stock of nappies– occupied so much space.

Rory had started his part-time schedule in his role as a probation officer and was becoming more involved in the community pub project. He was exploring the possibility of building a community partnership and applying for funding grants for such projects. The village of Hawes in Yorkshire provided a potential model in how to set up and sustain such an arrangement. They had control and responsibility for various village projects, including the local pub, a shop and the petrol station, all providing vital services to support and maintain village life.

The Stag Inn was doing well and was now open six nights per week under the stewardship of the young and enthusiastic ex-army couple who had taken on the role of managing the pub. They had both served in the REME and had a range of transferable skills, including mechanical expertise.

Marcus and Hayley had managed to fit into the community very well from the start and readily bought into the concept of a community venue. Not that dissimilar to the idea of the regimental family in the army, as they regularly pointed out. A quiz night and an open mic sing along were already established as popular events and the shop was also taking shape. The idea of an 'exchange facility' had proved to be popular, with villagers bringing their various garden produce and swopping items in 'the shop'. A book lending service had also been established for a nominal fee of £1 per lend. As they had anticipated, this arrangement only needed nominal oversight and did not need to be 'staffed' as such; it was a self-service arrangement.

Rory was well aware that they had been lucky in starting the project with some substantial help from influential and relatively wealthy local people but that, if the venture was to continue and develop further, it would need to secure other sources of funding. The scope for European funding had obviously diminished with the UK's decision to leave the European Union but other sources were available to assist and support rural life and Rory had several lines of enquiry in hand and, indeed, several ongoing applications.

Chapter Two

Emma was pleased that some members of the village seemed so genuinely delighted by the arrival of Poppy May and were keen to offer help and support. She wanted to strike a healthy balance between accepting some assistance and trying for the most part to learn to cope on their own. She was, however, enjoying the adjustment to the slower pace of rural life and feeling part of a community, in contrast to her previously frantic city existence.

Relations with her mother, although significantly improved, were still a little tense and difficult. Tentatively, Emma suggested to her mum that she might like to visit once a fortnight to help with the baby and that they could go shopping together. She was pleased that her offer seemed to be welcomed and seen as an attempt at building bridges, rather than previous attempts to keep her at arm's length.

The arrangement began with relative ease, with her mum enjoying some contact with her granddaughter, and a fortnightly shopping trip helped them both to manage the basic housekeeping. Conversation tended to be light and Emma was conscious that it was not only her who was adjusting to new circumstances as her mum, too, was trying to reconfigure her life after the sudden and unexpected loss of her husband.

She seemed to be coping better than Emma would have anticipated, as her dad had always appeared to be the dominant partner. Her mum would talk about having to find out and learn about taking more control in the management of her money, and things like insurance and servicing the car, but that she quite liked this new lease of life. She never mentioned any wish or intention to find a new partner. Emma felt open-minded about the prospect of her mum forming any new relationship, but it was very early days after all, and she accepted that rebuilding her life was up to her mum in her own way and in her own time.

It was after several months that, unexpectedly, her mum started to talk about the disclosure of Rory's adoption and the shock and impact on both him and Emma. This didn't exactly amount to an apology but Emma felt that there was some sense of acknowledgement about how badly both her mum and dad had handled the whole situation. Emma listened but didn't want to press the point before rescuing the situation by emphasising the obvious – that the revelation had at least allowed Rory to learn who he really was and for them to be free to become a couple, rather than all those years of feeling at odds with the status of brother and sister.

The sense of hurt was still strong for Emma but, on balance, she felt that she and Rory had been right not to become estranged from her mother completely.

Over the summer months, Emma was able to consolidate and develop her business to some degree around the demands of a young family. Rory's chickens had started to produce eggs and he had planted some vegetables in the garden. Any romantic notion of self-sufficiency was a long way off but it was fun to grow at least some of their own food.

Emma laughed sometimes at the contrasts in her new life; one minute changing nappies and the next answering a call from a client asking for business advice. The contrasts associated with motherhood were all too evident. She hoped that her clients understood if she suddenly appeared to have 'lost the plot' or be unduly distracted.

Chapter Three

Rory was very busy at work, trying to achieve the impossible in part-time hours. He was beginning to think that maybe running a caseload wasn't the best option in those circumstances... Maybe it was time to specialise within his role as a probation officer. Working in courts, prisons or programmes, for example, were all still options open to him.

Also, he found himself feeling more and more uncomfortable with the developing culture at work. The change in ethos within the organisation was becoming ever more difficult to reconcile with his values and those of the 'service' that he had originally joined. The wholesale change, since the creation of the National Probation Service in 2014, towards a more business-orientated focus did not sit easily with him. Not that Rory was anti-business, far from it. He had been brought up in a business family and had a sound understanding of its nature, which of course was helpful in supporting Emma. However, the clash of cultures between a service and a business ethos was becoming more of a critical issue for him.

So much of his work was now contracted to a labyrinth of private companies making the lines of communication and accountability become ever more complex. He remembered thinking at the time of its implementation how hopelessly flawed the new model was. Whoever thought that to abandon an integrated single national offender management service and create a two-tier system with twenty-one private companies operating services for 'medium and low risk offenders' would somehow enhance efficiency, communication and outcomes seemed to Rory to be completely misguided.

In the office the following day, conversation in the tea room reflected the same misgivings.

'Morning Rory, you OK?' asked Sophie Cooper, one of the other probation officers in the team at Upper

Lowbridge.

'Yes, fine thanks, Sophie...' Rory replied, unconvincingly.

'You look troubled, my friend,' posed Joseph Oba, another colleague.

'Oh Joseph, you are so perceptive. I'm just struggling at the moment with all these changes and the direction the service has taken.'

'Oh, aren't we all?' interjected Sophie. 'I've resisted thinking that things aren't what they used to be, but now there is no question; they are not. This is a far different service to the one I joined and, like you, I have grave misgivings about how it's performing, where it's heading and the likely consequences.'

'Hey, we still deal face-to-face with humanity in all its glory, don't we?' added Joseph.

'Joseph, you are so grounded, aren't you?' responded Rory. 'But how do you deal with all the politics?'

'Oh, I just ignore it, my friend. That's my approach,' Joseph replied, laughing as he walked away with his coffee.

Rory followed him to his desk and switched on his computer, only to be faced with the usual overwhelming number of messages, demands for instant information and long instructions that would be assumed to be assimilated and implemented the moment that they had been sent. Rory was used to working hard but an increasing sense of being overwhelmed was beginning to concern him. Some officers seemed to manage the workload, others clearly didn't. Morale generally was hardly buoyant – in fact, people were leaving and efforts to recruit new staff were faltering.

Rory started to prioritise some of the messages and quickly deleted the irrelevant, out of date or unimportant ones. One particular message grabbed his attention from yesterday's duty officer.

Matis Zukas called in to see you today, very distressed – see case record.

Rory remembered that Matis was on supervision for

knife-related crime.

His family came from Lithuania. His grandfather had been working in Poland when the Nazis invaded at the beginning of the Second World War and had managed to escape across Europe to Britain. He had joined the RAF and trained as a fighter pilot. He fought in the Battle of Britain in 1940, survived the war and had settled in England.

Matis was therefore the third generation of his family to reside in the UK and, although conscious of and proud of his Lithuanian heritage, he considered himself thoroughly British. He referred to himself as Mat, which felt right to him. His family had no previous experience of the British criminal justice system before he had got into trouble.

The recent wave of anti-immigration views and protests had affected him when some of his school friends started to reject him and he became the target for abuse and bullying. Eventually, Mat had taken matters into his own hands and gone to school armed with a knife in order to be able to defend himself, as he saw it.

When one of the staff intervened in a confrontation between Mat and his principal protagonist, it became apparent that Mat was carrying a knife. As a result, he was expelled from school and prosecuted for possession and threatening behaviour, resulting in a community supervision order.

Matis had responded well to supervision and had adapted to home tuition, albeit a very poor substitute to mainstream education. His parents were disappointed with the authority's response and were keen for him to complete his education. Matis was well-motivated and did manage to take some exams and secure a place at college on a general building trades course. His father was able to employ him in the family building firm and to give him the practical grounding to consider further training in any one of the building trades. As a result, Matis aspired to become an electrician.

Recently, Matis had reported a reoccurrence of negative

behaviour towards him based on the perception that he must be a foreign immigrant. He was subject to abuse and the accusation of 'taking our jobs'; at times the resentment risked turning into violence. Mat was acutely aware of the likely consequences should he choose to retaliate again in response to the provocation.

The case record indicated that he was struggling to contain his sense of anger at what was happening. He felt that some people were deliberately trying to provoke him into confrontation in order to get him into trouble and to claim justification for their slanted and prejudicial views.

Rory decided that he would ring the family home to try to get a sense of how bad things were and to offer some reassurance.

Sophie walked past his desk and stopped for a brief word.

'So, Rory, are you coping with all these negative feelings or are you going to do something about it?' she posed.

'Yes, I'm managing, Sophie, but it just feels so uncomfortable that I'm beginning to wonder how long I can stick this.'

'If you left, Rory, have you considered what else you might do?'

'That's part of the problem, Sophie. I'm not sure.'

'Is there scope in the work you are doing with the community project?' she asked.

'You mean could I do that full time?' he responded rhetorically. 'I suppose that maybe possible, but there's not much money in it!'

'Is money that important to you?'

'No, not really, only in the sense to have enough to live on,' he responded.

'Oh well, I wish you luck whatever you decide, but it would be a shame to see another good officer leave the profession. Have you talked to Laura about it in supervision?'

'No, not yet. Maybe I ought,' he replied.

'I think you should,' said Sophie as she moved on, heading for the photocopier.

Rory picked up the phone to ring the Zukas family home. It rang and a female voice answered.

'Hello, Zukas family builders. Can I help you?'

'Hello, Mrs Zukas, it's Rory Scott from probation. I understand that Matis called into the office yesterday? He was reported to be quite agitated. What's your view of the situation?'

'Oh, Rory, I'm glad you rang. Can you come and see us please, maybe one evening this week, to talk about it? I'm worried for him, really worried. He sees himself as British, as I am, and gets really incensed when people call him foreign, not that he's anti-foreigner at all. He seems to have quite a sense of justice, you see, and doesn't like what he perceives as unfairness. He is always helping other people.'

'He's not talking about, planning or anticipating violence, is he?'

'Oh no, I don't think so.'

'OK, Mrs Zukas. Wednesday is one of my late nights. I'll call in next week around six o'clock, if that's OK?'

'That would be great, Rory. Thank you. I'm sure he'd like to see you, and so would his father and I. All this is beginning to make his grandfather quite ill; he fears the return of extremism,' she started to say as Rory had to ring off to respond to another call.

The following day, Rory was due to see Laura, his manager for supervision, as part of the regular performance review process. Laura remained well-liked and respected by the team and Rory felt relatively comfortable with the prospect of sharing some of his feelings about his future in the service with her.

After she had raised various issues and they had reviewed a number of particularly high risk cases, Rory had his opportunity to express some of his concerns.

'Laura there is something I want to discuss with you. I'm increasingly finding myself at odds with the organisation and wondering how best to respond.'

'OK, Rory. You are not alone...' she responded quickly.

'I know that, Laura, but others seem to either cope better with their misgivings or just ignore the wider picture and get on with it.'

'Both being reasonable coping strategies, Rory. So, how far have you thought through how you might deal with these concerns?'

'I suppose it just grows on you. I'm still young in the service but already feeling that this is not the organisation that I signed up for. I don't like the political context: the blame culture, the lack of understanding and compassion that hails from government, the obsession with privatising services regardless of the poor outcomes and the increasingly ruthless tone that basically says "shut up and get on with it"!'

'Who says "shut up and get on with it", Rory?' Laura asked.

'Not you personally, Laura, but that seems to be the blanket attitude of the organisation these days. No consultation just dictum, more and more work and fewer and fewer staff with ever-diminishing terms and conditions of employment,' Rory replied, starting to get matters off his chest.

'What do you mean, Rory?'

'Come on, Laura, neither the government nor the service care about us and the attitude increasingly seems to be one of "you're lucky to have a job and if you don't like it others would be grateful",' responded Rory as he started to feel himself becoming frustrated.

'You sound quite angry, Rory.'

'Of course I'm bloody angry, I'm human...' he responded.

'OK, let's just calm down and get a sense of perspective. You work for an organisation, one you elected to join. True, as individuals, we do not direct it and there will always be things about it that we don't like and we work in an area that is highly politicised. Rory, you have mentioned this before, it's been a recurring theme for you over the last few years. It's a matter for you, ultimately. You're a good officer and you should be proud of that, but whether this is for you long term or not is a choice only you can make,' said Laura, trying to be both realistic and sensitive.

Rory hesitated.

'Rory, look, there is no hurry to try to resolve this, but please do consider it thoroughly before you make any decisions,' Laura continued.

'You mean the grass isn't always greener elsewhere?'

'Yes, there is that, but have you considered other areas of the service, Rory? You have previously expressed an interest in sex offender work in prison or delivering in programmes in the community,' said Laura, conscious of time and trying to end on a positive note.

'Yes, I have. Maybe it's just time for a change,' Rory postulated.

'Think about that – you would have a lot to offer either specialism if you decided to apply for a transfer. Come back to me if you want to discuss it further and keep me informed about how you are feeling. I want you on board, Rory. You are a big part of this team and you are very good at what you do, but I'll support you whatever you decide,' Laura concluded, sincerely hoping she had offered enough encouragement for him to stick with it.

Rory was by no means the only officer that she had encountered with similar reservations.

Chapter Four

'Do you fancy eating in The Stag tonight, Em?' asked Rory. Hopeful that he was about to leave for work.

'Yes, OK, Rory, but we'll need a babysitter, unless we go early doors?'

'Let's do that then. We'll leave when I get home, walk Bracken and end up at the pub. We can sit outside and then dog and baby won't bother anybody else.'

'OK, love, see you later,' concluded Emma, feeling pleased.

She walked over to Poppy in her bouncy chair to tell her all about it.

'Hey, Poppy, your lovely Daddy is going to take us all to the pub tonight for dinner!' she announced. 'Is that alright with you too, Bracken?' she asked, only to be greeted by a wagging tail.

Emma was due to attend a coffee morning at the pub later where some of the mums gathered on Wednesdays. Poppy would get loads of attention and she could extract the collective wisdom and advice of generations about her latest encounter with a new baby situation. After that, Emma anticipated making a few business calls before having a nap with Poppy prior to Rory coming home. Although Wednesday evening was usually his late night, Rory was expected home earlier that evening.

At work, Rory was thinking about following up Laura's advice and looking into a transfer to Stafford prison. He decided that he would ring the probation team there to get an inside view. Sophie had previously worked in both Drake Hall women's prison and at Featherstone adult male establishment near Wolverhampton, so he would consult her too.

Rory had two new cases allocated to him by the central allocation process. It was now just a numbers approach to distributing new cases, with no attempt to match offender to officer. *A long way*, he thought, *from the days when teams would discuss new cases and decide who would be the best match.* As Sophie reminded them, at least with this approach there was a better chance of a fairer distribution of work, with cases being allocated at random and numbers being fairly equal between officers. Sophie used to say that all sorts of games were played to manipulate allocation and some officers did tend to lead a charmed life at the expense of others. This approach was at least quick, simple and more efficient.

His two new cases were interesting: a transfer in from another area of a prisoner about to be released to one of the Staffordshire hostels and a female death by dangerous driving case at the start of her three year sentence. It was something of a freak accident, by all accounts.

Stacy Browning had been on her way to work early one morning in December last year. The weather was good and she was both sober and alert. A young mum, Mandy Carol, was making her way to work too, as a cleaner at the local pub, with her baby daughter Shell. The landlord was understanding and kind enough to let her bring Shell with her and clean the pub early well before opening time. He was sympathetic to a single parent trying to earn a living.

Stacy Browning was a solicitor working for the Crown Prosecution Service, based in Birmingham. She came from a wealthy background, had been privately educated, and was bright and ambitious. On that morning, Stacy was thinking about the new boyfriend she had recently met, an accountant from a prestigious Birmingham firm. They were due to meet that evening for dinner and Stacy was considering whether it was the right time to agree to stay overnight at his penthouse flat. She had packed a bag in anticipation.

As she drove out of the town, from Upper Lowbridge towards the motorway, she gathered speed in her bright red sports car. Approaching the motorway junction, the road narrowed. A dog had suddenly run across the road in front of her and she had turned sharply to avoid it but, in doing so, she had temporarily lost control of the vehicle and hit the kerb. She had mounted the pavement and was headed straight for Mandy Carol as she emerged from around a corner, walking along that winter's morning, pushing her child's buggy in front of her.

Mandy looked up in horror and tried desperately to move away from the path of the fast approaching car. As she tried to move right, the car followed her and clipped the buggy before turning over and crashing through a hedge and landing upside down in a ditch. Mandy had been thrown to the ground. As Mandy looked up from where she lay, she could see that the pushchair and her precious daughter, were both trapped under the car, which by then was a steaming mangle of metal, glass and plastic crumpled into the mud of a farmer's field.

Rory read the official account of the accident, the police charges, the probation court report and the sentencing judge's comments. It was both harrowing and tragic. A lost young life, a bereaved mother, a responsible young driver with so much promise who now faced imprisonment rather than a professional career and a potential new romance. The case had attracted considerable media attention, with Stacy having been subjected to death threats, and it was anticipated that managing her sentence would continue to be high profile, risky and subject to continued media interest.

He would need to find which prison she had been sent to and visit as soon as he could.

Chapter Five

Passers-by had stopped and had gone to Mandy's aid only to find a mother totally distraught, knowing the worst. An elderly lady tried her best to calm and comfort her whilst others rang the emergency services. Both an off-duty police officer and a firefighter had stopped to lend their expertise and start to coordinate the rescue effort and instigate some traffic control.

The firefighter then turned his attention to investigate the upturned car. To a man of many years' experience, the degree of violence and damage involved in a major car crash was still a shocking experience, and this was no different. As he approached the vehicle, the full horror of the situation was immediately evident to him – a child was involved, an infant. He could identify the remnants of a push chair intertwined with the wreckage of the car. As he braced himself to look further, an ex-soldier who had also stopped to help was stood by his side. He was a man with hardened battle experience in Afghanistan as a medic.

As they exchanged knowing glances, they peered into the remains of the chair together to see the shocking impact of trauma on such a young child. They both knew from experience that there was no chance of saving the baby as they turned their attention to the remaining framework of the car.

Help began to arrive with several ambulances and more firefighters, who brought with them cutting equipment. As they tried to assess what was in front of them, unexpectedly the driver spoke.

'I don't think I'm trapped. I think I'm OK,' Stacy said quietly.

The two men and the professionals who were now gathered round could hardly believe what they had just heard, given the state of the car, but were relieved nevertheless.

It soon became apparent that there was only one

occupant in the vehicle, so they were able to quickly help Stacy to climb out of the car and get to a waiting ambulance.

The crews and the passers-by said their goodbyes and expressed their thanks as they parted, each to resume their normal lives and responsibilities.

***

Remarkably, Stacy was relatively unhurt in the accident. Her car was well designed to protect her and had saved her from serious injury. As she sat in the police station, she thought of the night that she had been expecting, was hoping for, and the night she now faced in a police cell. She thought of the bag that she had packed, of the flimsy nightwear and underwear that she had taken with her and how inappropriate it all was now.

Stacy knew that the child couldn't possibly have survived the impact of the crash, and she tried to imagine the effect on the poor young mother. Stacy had an image stuck in her mind of the horror on her face as Stacy first saw her emerging from round that corner before the impact. Stacy was conscious that her life had now changed forever but felt that this was nothing compared to the situation faced by the grieving young mother.

As a lawyer, Stacy had a pretty good idea what was to come. She realised that, in the circumstances, death by dangerous driving was the likely outcome and, if convicted, that a prison sentence would inevitably follow. Her career was all but over and her life in tatters, she thought as she buried her head in her hands and started to cry.

By the time the officers came to interview her, she was calm. They asked her if she was ready to answer some questions and if there was anyone she would like to contact.

Stacy looked up and said meekly, 'Yes please. I would like to ring my parents.'

'OK, ma'am, we'll facilitate that. You may also like to consider whether you wish to contact a lawyer,' the officer said sympathetically.

'No, that won't be necessary,' Stacy replied.

'Are you sure, ma'am?'

'Yes, because I am one,' she replied and paused. 'I am a prosecutor for the CPS.'

'Oh, I see, ma'am. Well, we deal with all sorts here. You can, of course, in effect represent yourself but, if at any time you feel that you need an independent advisor, just ask, OK?' said the officer, obviously surprised by the situation.

***

As Rory finished reading the case papers it was obvious that Stacy Browning had eventually accepted full responsibility for the incident. Initially, she had tried to suggest other causes of the accident but the police report, witness statements and Mandy Carol's testimony all suggested very clearly where culpability lay. The sentencing judge had taken all the circumstances into account and three years seemed a consistent outcome to Rory compared with other similar cases that he had dealt with. Nevertheless, for the harm caused, it seemed completely at odds with other responses to taking a life. *Why were driving offences dealt with so differently to other offences of violence?* he wondered. Yes, usually there was no intent but the level of irresponsibility appeared to be of a similar nature to that occurring in other such violent offences.

Rory had to put his personal thoughts to one side and stay professional, however. He felt well prepared to meet her as he rang Foston Hall prison, near Uttoxeter, where he understood that she was being held, to make an appointment.

Chapter Six

A chaotic lifestyle continued to be a consistent aspect of life for the three Howell brothers, as it was for their parents, Bronwen and Glyn. Rhys Howell had received some disturbing news. His brother Elis, who was still in custody serving a life sentence, had written to him. Contact between the two brothers had become less frequent over the years and it had been awhile since Rhys had heard anything from Elis.

Amongst his random ramblings lambasting 'the system', Elis had commented that their mother, Bron, had visited him recently and looked terrible. He said that she had a black eye and some facial bruising. In his words, Elis had concluded:

'Well, you know, Dad always used to batter her, Rhys. It looks like he's at it again, the bastard. He wouldn't be doing that if I was out, I can tell you!'

Rhys was shocked. No he didn't know that his mother was or had ever been subject to domestic violence. This came as a real jolt. Rhys had to acknowledge that he had never been terribly sympathetic towards his mother or her situation and had tended to blame her, along with his father, for his own deprived and poor background. He remembered his father being absent on many occasions and being an inconsistent and unreliable provider. He remembered that he could be moody and uncommunicative, that he was often distant and unhelpful, but he was sure that he hadn't either witnessed or experienced violence at his hand.

How odd, Rhys thought; if Elis was right, then both his mother and his father had managed to keep this from him for all those years. How odd that Elis claimed to know but had not said anything, not to him at least. Had Elis confronted their father, unbeknown to him, and was that part of the reason Elis was so angry? After all, Rhys remembered that Elis used to worship his dad as a boy.

Was the reality, once discovered, too much to take? he wondered.

This had the potential to change his whole perception, he thought. Maybe it was time to reconsider why his mother always seemed so subdued and apathetic, and why she drank so much. Maybe living with fear, threat and violence was behind her demise?

This was starting to raise some serious and difficult questions for Rhys at a time in his life when he thought that he had dealt with his negative feelings about his past. Maybe he had got it all wrong and had completely misjudged the situation? Suddenly Rhys was really not sure at all.

He paced up and down then went to make some tea, still feeling quite disoriented by these sudden revelations. After a while, Rhys paused and sat back, starting to consider how best to respond to this new situation. Although he was tempted to go straight to Porthmadog to confront his father and give him 'a dose of his own medicine', he reasoned that would not really be helpful. Then Rhys leaned back in his chair and laughed; he couldn't remember the last time he felt so aligned with his brother, Elis, as he felt sure that was exactly what he would have done if he was free to do so.

No, that wouldn't be appropriate, but maybe he could offer his mother sanctuary, he thought.

***

The coffee morning went well and, as anticipated, Poppy received all the attention. This was nice on one level, but Emma still found it all a little overpowering. There were one or two women in the group who she felt a real rapport with, people with whom she would be comfortable to share a confidence with. Some of the others, however, reminded her of some of the narrow-minded and self-obsessed people she used to work with. People whose sole focus seemed to be on their material existence, competitive people who were never satisfied.

'Wouldn't it be great to be able to set up your own community?' Emma posed to Hannah, one of the women she liked.

'What do you mean, Emma? Like setting off to the moon or something?' she replied, feeling amused and wondering where that idea had come from.

'No, I mean if you had the chance to start anew, to start afresh, how might that feel?'

'Like after some grand natural disaster or something?'

'No, Hannah, nothing like that, not emerging from the ashes following an earthquake or something, but just choosing to set up a new life in a different place – to set up a community from scratch.'

'You're weird, Emma Scott, do you know that? You really are!' Hannah replied.

Maybe I am, she thought.

'What are you two looking so intense about?' asked one of the other women.

'Oh, nothing,' Emma replied, quickly changing the subject. 'While I have you all here, can I glean some collective advice about managing a baby's sleeping patterns?'

Well, that certainly concentrated their minds for the rest of the morning, leaving Emma with a whole heap of contradictory experiences and suggestions to consider!

Rory was ploughing his way through enquiries and endless information, trying unsuccessfully to feed the incessant demands of the ever-present computer. He was covering the role of duty officer, which was adding to the pressures of the day on top of an existing busy schedule, but he was determined to finish reasonably early, to be able to get home to his family, as promised, that evening.

Emma and Poppy enjoyed their little nap in the afternoon. Emma woke first and was able to leave Poppy to sleep on for a while. She thought again about her conversation in the morning about creating a different life. It intrigued her. Emma considered that she and Rory had managed to recast their relationship to something that they both wanted, something that was not possible until they had discovered that they weren't blood relatives after all. She had realigned her business interests, Rory had made adjustments to his working arrangements as well, with two very different part time commitments, so it was possible. *Why couldn't we take the idea further?* she thought, as she determined to discuss it with Rory when he got home.

Despite his best efforts, Rory was struggling at work to complete everything that he had started that day. By six o'clock, he resolved to leave anyway. He'd been there since eight that morning, with no break all day. He'd had the occasional drink at his desk and had munched his sandwich at the computer. He hadn't managed to leave the office. As he left, however, others were still working.

As he drove home, Rory couldn't help but think that it shouldn't be like this. There was simply insufficient staff to cover the workload. He tried to switch his mind, however, away from work and forward to pleasant thoughts of home and family; his lovely wife and daughter, of whom he was so proud and with whom he shared his life.

The traffic wasn't too heavy as he left the main road and headed back home to Coppermere through the country lanes. The ancient farm routes through the countryside were edged by traditional hawthorn hedges. The green fields always helped him to separate thoughts of work and home. The space, the countryside and the village were all therapeutic, he thought. As he reached the edge of the village, Rory could sense the anticipation of approaching home as he drove past the church and the pub to arrive safely at The Old School House.

He could hear Bracken barking as he opened the front door, and he was met by a wagging tail and excitement.

'Hello, love,' Emma called from the kitchen, where she was desperately trying to organise something for dinner the following day, whilst watching Poppy.

'Oh, I see you have help!' Rory remarked as he joined

them.

'Yes, bless her...Have you had a good day?'

'It was another long and busy day, that's for sure, love. I'm still young. I don't know how the older officers cope with it all. Some of them look so tired. I do wonder how realistic it will be for people to sustain careers in this area of work, or indeed most others through their fifties and sixties, let alone beyond that...'

'That's interesting. I had some thoughts today that I wanted to share with you. Anyway, come in first. Tea?' Emma invited.

'Oh, yes please,' Rory replied as he lifted Poppy out of her cot.

Bracken continued to chase up and down, relentlessly pointing to his lead hanging by the coats.

'Yes, I know, Bracken. It won't be long,' Rory reassured him.

After he had finished his cup of tea, Rory got changed while Emma wrapped Poppy up in a sleepsuit and placed her in the pushchair so they were ready to go. Rory grabbed Bracken's lead as they left the house, heading for a pleasant evening's stroll.

They walked together through the village to a footpath that they often used. Rory let Bracken off the lead and Emma easily managed the pushchair on the even path. It followed the side of the churchyard and across a field towards the hotel venue where they had got married. It was a well-maintained path and a popular area for dog walkers.

Rory and Emma walked on and stopped at the top of the hill to enjoy the view across the fields. They held hands for a moment and kissed while Poppy was singing along to herself and Bracken was chasing sticks.

'It is a lovely spot here, isn't it, Rory?'

'Yes, love, it certainly is.' Rory paused and continued, 'You wanted to share some thoughts?'

'Yes, yes, I did. I was thinking today about our lives and where the future might take us, Rory, and I had this idea of starting a new community, like a new village from scratch; choosing who you might live with and selecting a suitable place, selecting a place to put down roots and to raise our family.'

'OK, isn't that here then?' he replied.

'Well, no, not exactly. I love the house and I like the village, but I just thought this idea could go further. That's all.'

'The perfect community, isn't that a little idealistic?'

'Oh yes, maybe it is, but why not dream?'

'Is it a dream, Em, or are you really looking to make this happen?' asked Rory, thinking that he knew her likely answer.

Emma smiled and moved in closer to him, looking deeply into his eyes.

'I'd really like to explore this idea, Rory, and I'd really like to explore it with you.'

Bracken ran past with a huge stick in his mouth and bashed into the pushchair, making Poppy cry, and the moment was lost.

Emma comforted her while Rory broke the stick down to a manageable size and threw it for Bracken to chase. They walked on a little further as Rory's phone rang with a call from work. It was Laura wanting to ask him to cover for her briefly on his first morning the following week while she attended a meeting. She also mentioned that she had heard that a vacancy was coming up at Stafford Prison, if he was interested.

Rory agreed to cover for her and listened while she explained a couple of things that she wanted him to do for her. His mind switched, however, to the prospect of a move to the prison. He was excited and looked forward to making some enquiries the next day.

Emma sensed that it was work and had walked on, pushing Poppy and chattering to her about the trees and the birds while Bracken just ran everywhere.

'Emma, that was Laura. She's heard that a vacancy might be coming up at the prison. I may want to go for it. It would be exciting, a change and easier to manage on part time hours, I think.'

'OK, Rory,' she replied. 'You do what you think is right.' She was a little disappointed that her dream conversation had ended prematurely, but still wondered if she had managed to plant a seed nevertheless.

When they arrived at the pub, it was actually quite busy, which was good to see. They said their hellos to the villagers as Emma selected a table outside and positioned Poppy, who was sound asleep by then, safely in the shade. Rory went to fetch some menus and a drink while Bracken found the dog water bowl for himself.

Rory returned with a fruit juice with soda for Emma and a pint of Titanic Steerage for himself. Whilst Emma was breastfeeding, she was being careful about what she drank.

'That was a lovely walk, Rory,' Emma remarked. 'It's so nice at this time of year to be able to get out in the light summer evenings, and it's some fresh air for Poppy.'

'Good, glad you enjoyed it. What do you fancy to eat?' he replied.

They sat and shared their respective experiences of the day. Rory talked about feeling exhausted and washed out after his three day stint at probation. He expressed some sense of satisfaction about what he had managed to achieve, but also anxiety about what was inevitably left undone.

Emma told him about the coffee morning, the other women and their thoughts about helping to manage Poppy's sleep pattern. She briefly referred to her exchange with Hannah, who obviously thought that she was mad. Rory nodded but she could tell he was not really listening. He looked so tired.

They tucked into their meals, which were freshly cooked and well received. They had both selected the daily special, which that night was an Italian chicken and tomato dish with pasta. Rory had another pint while Bracken sat in hope of any leftovers. Emma could see Rory's mind was wandering. She looked at him as if to ask what he was thinking.

'I do wonder, Em, what the future holds. I do get concerned about some of the bigger issues facing the country, and indeed humanity. The world so often now seems a restless and insecure place for so many people. What sort of a world will we leave for our children, Em?' Rory posed, suddenly feeling philosophical.

Emma smiled. He may not have recognised it yet, but she knew that the seed had been planted!

Chapter Seven

At work over the next few days, Rhys kept going over his thoughts and memories in relation to Elis's revelation about their mother's experience of domestic violence. Snippets of thoughts and memories came back to him.

He didn't remember seeing his mother bruised, but all those times that she would spend two or three days in bed saying she had the flu and he thought that she was just drunk – was it that she was recovering from an assault and hoping to hide the evidence? Was she actually trying to protect her brood rather than neglect it? Had she taken the blows when he and his brothers had got into trouble, which they did regularly? Was she in fact more of a hero than a villain?

Rhys could remember shouting and angry words in the household but, at the time, thought that was just normal. Maybe it was normal for them, but it shouldn't have been. It was only recently that he had reflected and accepted that this was not a healthy environment in which to bring up children. An image flashed through his mind; *yes, that winter's day when I came home early from school*, he remembered. *I was only about six and had wet myself at school and didn't want to tell the teacher, so I left early at break time and just walked home, hoping to get myself sorted out without anyone knowing. I didn't want to get into trouble*, he thought.

Rhys remembered walking in on his mum and dad at home. He remembered his mum's red face and, at the time, he had thought it was just the flush of winter chill on her skin, but maybe it wasn't. He remembered his father storming off that day and not coming back for days as his mother desperately tried to keep the family going on her own.

So what can I do now? Rhys thought to himself. *I can't just leave her in this situation. I can't realistically resolve it after all these years. Father is not going to change now.*

No, he'll probably become even more cantankerous. Confronting him wouldn't solve anything either. No, the answer is obvious, he thought; *I need to rescue her.*

Chapter Eight

Rory woke early, looking forward to his two days working for the pub and community partnership. He was due to meet Edward, the project's solicitor, later that day. They were due to discuss progress with grant applications and partnership arrangements, along with reviewing the project's financial position at this early stage.

Poppy had been awake for a while so, after a feed, Rory took her with him to leave Emma to have some more sleep. It was six o'clock as he sat Poppy in the bouncy chair and put the kettle on. Bracken waited in anticipation.

'You may have to wait a while, Bracken, but you can come with me to meet Edward later,' Rory explained as if Bracken could fully understand. He had agreed to work at home in the afternoon with Poppy to give Emma a break and just take herself off to town to be a young woman for a while and not just a mum. Emma had said that she would go to Newport and wander round the shops and have a coffee in one of the nice little cafes.

A certain odour signalled the need for a nappy change as Rory started to order his papers on the kitchen table for the forthcoming meeting. He was excited about the potential in the project but also conscious of the risks. They had managed to secure sufficient financial backing to get through the first six months, but there would come a point where their level of turnover and profit would become critical.

Rory changed Poppy's nappy while Bracken looked on, not quite knowing what to make of this new arrival who seemed to take up so much time and create such a range of interesting smells.

Rory let his faithful friend out into the garden to do what dogs do as he placed the well-wrapped contents of Poppy's latest production in the bin. Bracken was safe to leave out in the garden for a moment while he set about tidying up the kitchen and making some breakfast. Rory knew Emma would appreciate a nice fresh-boiled egg when she emerged.

Later, he set off with Bracken to meet Edward at the pub.

'Hi, Rory, how are you?' Edward enquired, noticing the heavy look in his eyes.

'I'm OK, Edward, just could do with a little more sleep, that's all,' he replied.

'Don't worry. It won't seem like five minutes before she's setting off to go to school! They grow up so fast, Rory. Just try to enjoy every minute.'

'Did you always enjoy your children, Edward?' Rory enquired.

'No, of course not, but mostly yes I did. They are all independent now, with their own families.'

'You did a good job then?'

'I like to think so!'

The two men sat down outside in the sunshine to look at their progress and plans.

'OK, Rory, current situation first then, how does our financial picture look at this point?' said Edward decisively 'Then we can look at future plans.'

Rory described the breakdown of current costs against revenue. At this stage, neither of the men were surprised to find that they were in deficit. However, early revenue figures were encouraging. It had been made clear to Marcus and Hayley, the new publicans, from the start that they would need to grow the business fairly quickly if their contract was to be confirmed after the initial six month period. Both agreed that the couple had shown enterprise and initiative and been readily accepted by the local community. Several events were planned for the future, which had potential to generate good returns.

Rory was able to report that the local tradesmen had turned their attention to the pub garden and created a really pleasant seating area and lawn with an outdoor pizza oven and barbeque facility. Hayley was busy organising a celebration featuring some local people offering to sing and perform live. A group of youngsters had formed the beginnings of a band and were keen to try out the limited range of songs that they had practiced so far. The lead singer was something of a star by all accounts. There was also a jazz band in the village made up of residents who had played live for many years at local events and gatherings. It promised to be a good night and Hayley hoped to attract visitors from outside the area.

Marcus was in negotiation with a local land owner to run a car boot sale on a field adjacent to the pub and some early investigations suggested that the idea of setting up a caravan-certified location was feasible. Investment would be needed to establish limited facilities, including electrical hook up for five vans, access to water and rubbish collection, together with use of the toilet facilities in the pub. A designated shower could be a later consideration. A steady series of visitors would hopefully patronise the pub and its shop/exchange as well as generate a rental income.

Potential sources of grant aid had become more difficult to access in the light of the UK's plans to leave the European Union, but Rory was exploring UK-based funds and sponsorship arrangements. Also, the local book club, the WI, a mother and toddler group and an open coffee morning twice per week had all booked the use of the main pub room in the mornings for a modest fee.

Edward was pleased with progress and promised to report back to Sam the chairman that evening.

'Well done, Rory. That's encouraging and a good start. Do pass on our thanks to Marcus and Hayley too. Right, I'd better get back to work. See you later,' said Edward as he set off towards his car.

Bracken looked up as if to say "have you finished now and can we have a walk" and he readily agreed, gathering up his papers. They set off in the warm summer breeze along the more circuitous way back to the house. Rory was buzzing with ideas and keen to make some progress at home that afternoon, if Poppy allowed him the opportunity!

***

Rhys thought how he might help his mother. He thought about helping her to set up a viable independent existence away from the influence and threat posed by his father, Glyn. He thought about inviting her to move nearer to him. Either way, he felt that, at this point, he had a moral duty to take her away from the threat of violence and to give her some comfort and security at this stage in her life. It was something that he felt he both wanted and needed to do. Duty was one motivation but, although it surprised him, he also felt a strong desire to help her. However, he had to be realistic – Glyn could be a formidable adversary, one who had largely left him alone for some while. He didn't want to antagonise him and awake the beast within. *Could I achieve both?* he wondered.

Rhys started to look at housing solutions in his own area, their application criteria and costs. He looked at how much he could realistically contribute and what it might be reasonable to expect his mother to provide for herself. He had no family of his own, after all, and was on a good salary. Rhys had felt uncomfortable for some time with the notion that he actually earned far more than he really needed. He spent several weeks researching various options until he paused for thought one Friday afternoon at work. *What am I doing?* he thought to himself. I learn that my mother is in imminent danger and I'm messing about here. I need to go and rescue her NOW!

The more he thought about it, the more absurd his position appeared. Why had he delayed taking action? It was four thirty in the afternoon, he had worked hours over his contracted time for many years. What was he waiting for? Go now, he told himself.

So, at four thirty-five, Rhys Howell left his desk and set off for North Wales. He set off on a journey he never thought he would make again – back to where he originated, back to all those negative memories that he recalled and hoped he had left well behind him – but the pull was stronger than ever to return. It was unfinished business – call it destiny, call it what you like – but he knew that he just had to do this and to do it now.

As he drove out of Liverpool that evening through the weekend traffic, he felt so destined, so determined, that Rhys really thought that nothing could distract him or change his plan to extract his mother from the hell that he now felt convinced that she had been living in for all these years. Part of him felt guilty that he had not acted before, that he didn't know the truth – or was it that he had chosen to ignore it for all these years? He was not sure.

Rhys drove out of the city towards the motorway and on towards Chester and the A55 coastal road to North Wales. Yes, he would sit down with his mother and consult her on what she wanted. Yes, they would have a sensible adult conversation, he thought, perhaps the only sensible adult conversation that they had ever had. He would lay out the options for her, the pros and cons, the consequences, and then leave her to decide. Yes, that would be for the best, he reasoned.

Rhys reached the start of the coastal section of the A55 heading towards Bangor and south onward to Porthmadog. He didn't want to stop, to be distracted or diverted from his task; this was the right thing to do, he felt convinced of that. The sea looked calm and inviting as he passed through the tunnels cut out of sheer rock. The evening was light and dry as he drove on, ever closer to his home area, a place that he had determined never to return to – a place that held such strong negative memories for him.

As he passed Bangor and the two bridges across to Anglesey, his mind rolled through images from his past, images of him and his two brothers as children, images from school. He thought of scrapes, fights and criminal behaviour that they had indulged in together. He thought about David, who had died on the mountain, he thought about Afan, who had tragically taken his own life, and he thought about the direction his own life had taken. A direction out of deprivation, depravity and poverty, a life renewed, a life reinvented, a life salvaged from the grinding inevitability of intergenerational chaos and failure.

Rhys continued down the North Wales coast, past Caernarfon on the A487,before turning off to Porthmadog.

After stopping briefly for a cup of tea to attempt to stabilise his nerves, Rhys drove into Porthmadog, along familiar streets that had not changed much since his memories as a child. He drove straight to the house where he remembered being brought up. He parked opposite, walked up to the front door and pushed the bell.

Not surprisingly on reflection, the person who opened the door was not his mother but a young woman with a baby who lived in the house now and had no knowledge of a Bronwen Howell or where she might be now.

Of course she wasn't there, but where is she? And who would know? Rhys asked himself. *It was eight fifteen by now, so none of the agencies who might know her would still be available to ask at this time*, he thought, *except perhaps one*. The agency that attracted all the shit jobs when everyone else had fallen away, the agency that was available 24/7 every day of the year – including Christmas Day, the agency that perhaps he was least likely to ask: the police.

Rhys knew where the police station was, or at least where it used to be, having spent many unhappy hours there in his youth. He smiled as he envisaged walking in to meet the same old desk sergeant that used to deal with him. No, he would be long retired by now and it would be some civilian on duty behind a glass screen, he thought to himself as he walked back to his car.

What next? Dare he approach the police? Questions and doubts ran through his mind as he started up the engine and moved off back towards the centre of town. He pulled over to park along the main street. *Is it worth asking in somewhere neutral like a pub?* he thought.

Rhys got out and started walking along the street. He didn't see anyone he knew –in fact, not much was familiar to him. He noticed a pub, one that he remembered, and wandered in. This was where he had first started underage drinking and used to sit by the window to see the local copper well before he got there, so he could finish his drink and nip out the back door. He stood just staring at the same seat and through the same window, almost expecting that same copper to suddenly appear, but he didn't. He wasn't there, of course. Not anymore.

An old man approached him. 'Rhys? Rhys Howell? We haven't seen you in these parts for a long time,' posed the man, almost suspiciously.

Rhys looked at him, trying to gain some glimmer of recognition, but none was forthcoming.

'Yes, I'm Rhys,' he said limply.

'You don't remember me, do you, son?' replied the old man.

'No, I'm sorry...'

'Mr Williams, I ran the local shop that you and your brothers used to try to steal from.'

'Oh, I'm sorry, Mr Williams,' Rhys replied, floundering, suddenly feeling embarrassed. 'Um, how much do I owe you?' he spluttered.

The old man laughed. 'It's a bit late for that now!'

'Let me at least buy you a drink,' Rhys offered, seeing the old man's glass was nearly empty.

'OK, you can do that, son,' said the old man as he looked around and announced, 'Look boys, Rhys Howell, return of the prodigal son, and he's buying!'

People looked up and laughed. At one time everyone would have known the Howell family.

'What brings you back, Rhys?' asked another old man.

'Actually, I've come looking for my mum.'

The pub fell silent and Rhys looked at all the faces directed at him.

'You should have been here a long time ago, Rhys, if

you cared about your mother,' said one voice.

'I was at school with her,' said another.

'Terrible life she's had,' said an elderly lady.

'I know. I'm sorry. Where is she now, does anyone know?' Rhys asked, feeling the glare of all those eyes.

'It'll take more than feeling sorry now, Rhys. She needed protecting from that bastard Glyn years ago, but nobody cared, nobody ever did anything to help her. She just took it, Rhys, and did her best to look after you three boys, not that her best was really good enough. You all went off on the wrong path, didn't you?' said Mr Williams.

'Yes, we did, I know, but I'm here now. I don't expect you to believe me, but I didn't know about the violence that she had suffered for all those years until Elis told me in a letter recently. I'd always blamed her, you see, that's why I broke away. That's why I never came back.'

'So, why are you here know, flashing your new money? What do you want, Rhys Howell?' said Mr Williams pointedly.

'I want to help her,' said Rhys, trying to sound as convincing as he could.

***

The pub fell silent again, as the regulars looked at each other in disbelief, until Mr Williams broke the silence.

'You're right, Rhys Howell, I don't believe you,' he said with feeling.

'This is an honest hard working community here, not helped by the likes of you. Your poor mother had a bad start in life, as you did, I suppose, but you and your brothers let this community down, Rhys. You hurt people, you conned people and you broke their trust. Glyn, I'll grant you, was the worst of men, and no doubt still is, wherever he is now. He does as he always did, wander about running and hiding from one person or another who he has taken for a ride, until he comes back and takes out all his frustrations on your mother. You're not welcome here, Rhys Howell,' he said, quietly but firmly, as others nodded their approval.

Rhys took the barbed comments, he listened – it hurt but he knew that it was true. He looked around the bar for expressions of support but found none.

'OK, Mr Williams, I can't argue with a word that you have said. I accept it. I can only apologise, however hollow that apology sounds to you, to all of you. Yes, I feel guilty, but I can't change the past, but maybe I can do something to improve the future. I came here with several ideas. One was to set my mum up in a new home, here in her own community amongst people that she knows, but now I'm not sure that would be right. Would it be good enough? Would it be safe? I doubt it. In short, she needs to move away – if she wants to, that is.'

'So what are you saying? That you have turned up here acting like a knight in shining armour to whisk your mother off to safety and security in your "castle" in Liverpool? If that's where you are…Is that it?' responded Mr Williams.

'Look,' said Rhys, casting his eyes around the room, 'I can't satisfy your wish to reject me, nor do I expect to. I can only say that I've moved on and tried to make something of my life and to do some good, which in a small way may help redress some of the hurt that I and my family have done. If you are willing to assist me in finding her, I promise that I will help her.'

A long silence followed, then muttering as the regulars turned to talk amongst themselves, before one of them asked, 'What about your father, Glyn? The authorities have never dealt with him properly. He can't just get away with it. What should we do about Glyn Morgan?'

'He could be anywhere across the whole of North Wales or the Welsh Marches. We don't even know where he is!' said another.

'What would you suggest, Rhys, with all this learning you've been telling us about?' challenged Mr Williams.

'I don't know, honestly I don't know. I could try to find him and have it out with him, but do you really think that would help? No, my priority now is to secure my mother's safety. Where is she? Between you someone must know?' replied Rhys, making one last-ditch effort.

'Whatever you do, Rhys, if you take her away from here that won't be the last of it, you realise. Glyn won't just let her go – he will come looking for you both,' warned Mr Williams.

'I'll worry about that later, at least she would be safe for now,' he replied.

'I know where she lives,' replied the elderly lady as she stood up and looked Rhys directly in the eye.

'If I tell you where she lives, will you do as you say, Rhys? Tell me honestly.'

It was as if her stare pieced him through to his very soul. How could he possibly do other than respond to her honestly, he thought.

'I'm not going to win your trust, I don't deserve it, but I do want to help. That's all I can say,' he said, looking straight back into the elderly lady's eyes.

'OK, Rhys, I'll tell you. The last I heard, she was living in one of the flats. I'll write the address down for you. You'll know where it is.'

***

The informal meeting quickly broke up, with people getting on with their own business. Amongst the dirty looks, there were a few good wishes at least as Rhys took the written note from the lady and left in search of the address.

The lady was right; he did know where this was. In his day about the most notorious council flats in the area, traditionally, they would get the last places on the list; the council would offer only the places you would accept if you were absolutely desperate. He remembered some really rough sorts who used to live there.

Rhys drove out of the town. By now it was ten o'clock. Not the best of visiting hours, nor a good time to go into the area in question, he thought. But it wasn't far. As he approached the estate, Rhys could see at a glance that it hadn't changed. Dogs roamed free, rubbish lay scattered all around and people lurked in dark shadows. Some of the flats he assumed must have been vacant as they had broken windows and looked in disrepair.

He pulled up, cautiously looking for somewhere to park, preferably under a street light. Rhys felt a real sense of fear, not one that he had encountered for a good while. *Will my wheels, or the car itself, still be there on my return?* he wondered.

He got out of the vehicle slowly, trying not to attract attention. He turned and looked across the street, scanning the area for potential trouble. Nothing obvious occurred to him as he turned to approach the block where number sixteen, a first floor flat, was located. The front door to the block was already ajar.

Rhys pushed through the gap and started to climb the stairs. His senses were alert and he did not have a good feeling as he paused to listen, anticipating trouble. As he climbed the second flight of stairs, a door opened to one of the flats and a rough and scabby dog was unceremoniously kicked out into the night.

Rhys reached the front door of number sixteen and stood still for a moment to listen again. Still feeling distinctly uneasy and wondering whether this really had been such a good idea, he put his ear to the door. There was nothing, no obvious sound of occupation. No human voices, no television, no other sound. Nothing. He eased open the letter box to look inside as suddenly the door opposite opened and a woman emerged in front of him, making him jump.

'Looking for Bron, love?' she asked.

'Yes, I'm her son,' he replied.

'Really?' she said in disbelief. 'You won't find her here, love. She's gone.'

'Gone? Gone where?' Rhys enquired, starting to feel really worried.

'To hospital I should think, judging by the state of her as she left!'

'To hospital, what do you mean? What happened?' he asked, impatiently.

'There was a terrible fight earlier this evening, even worse than their usual rows. It's him, that Glyn bloke, rotten to the core he is, always was. Treated her terrible, he did, poor dear.'

'Which hospital?' Rhys asked, starting to feel desperate.

'Ysbyty Alltwen in Tremadog probably. Do you want to go in? I have a key,' the woman asked, looking towards the flat door.

'Yes, I think I'd better,' he replied.

The women unlocked the door for him and left telling him to just shut it behind him when he went. He cautiously pushed open the door to reveal bedlam. Broken crockery, glass, upturned furniture, paper hanging from the walls, bags of rubbish in the corridor. It was a total mess, a smelly total mess. *How could anyone live here?* he thought.

Rhys started to move between the rooms. Everything was broken, dirty or shabby. *How sad*, he thought, *after a life time to end up like this*. His sadness was also tinged with an element of guilt that he had ignored his mother for so long. Standing in her bedroom, he suddenly heard movement. He looked out into the hallway and saw the living room door open and a shadow dash across the corridor and into the kitchen, slamming the door.

Surprised, and more than a little alarmed, Rhys tried to regain his composure and moved towards the door. There was a commotion in the kitchen and he pushed the door open gently to see an open window leading to a flat roof and the shape of a man jumping the last few feet down to the ground before disappearing through the back gate.

Glyn. He was sure it had to be Glyn making his escape.

Chapter Nine

When Rory got back to the house, Emma was ready to go out. Poppy had been fed and Emma had expressed some milk just in case. Poppy was having a nap, looking clean, peaceful and angelic.

'OK, love, you go and take a break. Come back when you are ready. No hurry, we'll manage. Bracken is good with babies, aren't you, boy?' he said.

She smiled and left the boys to it.

'Right, Bracken, you settle down while I get on with some work.'

Bracken looked up as if to say "OK, if you must".

Rory laid out his papers and his notes from the meeting on the kitchen table and started to make some plans. There were letters to write, phone calls to make and notes to write up and circulate to the committee and the membership. He was also thinking of the potential opportunity at the prison.

Whilst Poppy remained asleep, it didn't take Rory long to complete his work from the morning's meeting. He was pleased to circulate a thorough progress report on the project and put some wheels in motion to take his various ideas for future expansion a little further.

Bracken was asleep too, curled up under Poppy's downstairs cot. Rory took the opportunity to phone the prison.

It was ringing and he was trying to keep calm and not get too excited.

'HMP Stafford, can I help you?'

'Yes, can you put me through to the probation department please,' he asked courteously. After several attempts, the line was connected.

'Probation.'

'Hi, it's Rory Scott, probation officer from Upper Lowbridge office. I'm looking at options for a job change and wanted to know more about your role in the prison.'

'OK, Rory, it's Penny Patel. We've met, haven't we?'

'Yes, I think so, Penny,' he replied, trying desperately to remember where and when.

'OK, Rory, I take it you've not done a secondment to prison before? Have you visited Stafford Prison?'

'No, Penny, I've not worked in a prison, but I have visited a few, including Stafford, for parole reports or general resettlement planning.'

'OK, so you have some idea. The main difference with secondment is that you are working attached to a different organisation, which has similar wider aims but a different role and sees things in a different way than you will be used to in probation.'

'I see. Is that threatening or enlightening then, Penny?'

'Um, I don't know about that. It's certainly challenging, and it's different. It's good experience and actually I quite like it. It's more predictable than work in the community. The role is narrower and clearer and that makes it less stressful. It's easier to control your hours. We generally don't do evenings or weekends. I think it's well worthwhile and a dimension of experience that enhances your understanding of the wider criminal justice system, helping you to develop your own practice. Having said that, it's no pushover Rory; there are some very difficult characters here and times are hard in the prison environment. It's like a cauldron of emotion all the time.'

'It sounds interesting, Penny,' Rory replied, feeling positive.

'It certainly is. Actually, I'm in the process of moving on, Rory, so a vacancy is likely to occur fairly soon. Think about it and come and see us here if you are interested. Anyway, I have to go now. I have a prisoner waiting for a parole interview.'

'Thanks, Penny, I will,' said Rory, feeling quite enthused and encouraged by what he had heard.

When next in the office, Rory took the opportunity to consult Sophie about her experience of secondment and she broadly endorsed what Penny had told him. Rory decided that he wanted to give it a try and would approach Laura and ask for formal consideration. An opportunity to visit the prison had also materialised, with requests for reports on another of his high risk offenders who was currently at HMP Stafford.

Rory felt confident that, if successful, a move to the prison would come at the right time to enhance his experience, provide a new challenge and help him consider his longer term prospects within the service, or indeed elsewhere.

Chapter Ten

Rhys had already decided that there was no way that his mother could return to the chaos left at the flat. He quickly collected what little was left and still salvageable from the debris and set off to visit the local hospital. *One carrier bag, not much for a lifetime*, he thought as he placed his mother's few belongings in the boot of the car.

It was past midnight and no time to visit a hospital so, preferring his car to the trashed flat, Rhys tried to get some sleep. His visit would have to wait until morning. He was familiar with the hospital at Tremodog from previous encounters. It was not far from Porthmadog but, while thoughts were flashing through his mind, he struggled to sleep.

He got up and left early, glad to be leaving Porthmadog. Driving along once familiar roads, he soon found himself drawing into the hospital car park.

Rhys reported to reception to enquire whether his mother was in fact a patient at the hospital and established that what her neighbour had told him was correct. He ascertained the ward number and followed the signs in the hope of finding his mother in at least a stable condition. As he walked through the corridors, Rhys suddenly realised just how long it had been since he had last seen her. He couldn't remember how many years it might be. He wondered how she might respond and, indeed, whether she would actually want to see him. Would she even recognise him? Were they never that close after all? Maybe he was being unrealistic in planning to 'rescue her' and take her to stay with him?

Feeling very uncertain of the reaction that awaited him, Rhys walked into his mother's ward. One of the nurses kindly confirmed which bed she was in and, after enquiring who he was, escorted him to the relevant bay.

'Good morning, Bronwen. Here's your son to see you,' the nurse announced, much to Bronwen's surprise.

She sat up in bed, thinking immediately of either Afan or Elis, then realising that was not possible. *Can it really be Rhys after all this time?* she wondered.

Rhys approached, still feeling very uneasy.

'Mum, it's me, Rhys,' he uttered, meekly trying not to show his distress at the shameful sight of the bruised and dishevelled form in front of him. 'I heard what happened so I've come to see you.'

Bron looked up through swollen eyes and looked hard at him before managing to speak.

'Rhys, is it really you?'

'Yes, Mum, it is.'

'Why, Rhys? Why now after all this time? Why come to see me now? Where have you been?' she enquired pitifully.

Rhys looked down at her, struggling to hold back tears.

'What can I say, Mum? I'm here now,' was all that he could muster.

'Well, then you'd better come in and sit down,' Bron replied, as if at home.

Rhys wanted to apologise but knew that it would only sound hollow.

'Mum, I hadn't forgotten you. It's been difficult for me too. Elis wrote to me. Honestly, Mum, I didn't know.'

'Know what?'

'About the violence, Mum.'

'Were you blind?' Bron snapped, regretting it instantly.

'Mum, I don't expect you to believe me, but it's the truth. I didn't know that he beat you. You managed to hide it so well over the years.'

'Elis knew, why didn't you?' she asked, pointedly.

'I don't know, Mum. Elis was older than me and more streetwise, or maybe I just didn't want to see it. There were so many things to deal with back then.'

'Elis knew because he made it his business to know. Did he tell you that he tried to stop Glyn once? He was only fourteen and Glyn fought him off and gave him a hell of a beating. He probably told you that it was the boys at school?' Bron told him boldly. 'That's what a son does for his mother, Rhys.'

Rhys recoiled, that hurt, but he knew that she was right. What could he say?

'Mum, I'm not here to go over the past, there's too much to say. I'm here now because I felt that you needed me.'

'It's a bit late to suddenly develop a sense of duty, isn't it?' she replied, looking straight at him, piercing him with her glare.

'OK, maybe I shouldn't have come. Would you prefer it if I left?' he asked.

'You mean just walk away and leave me again? No, I wouldn't choose it this way anymore than I expect you would, but you are all I have left now, so don't run, son. Stay with me,' said Bron and held out her withered hand.

Rhys took it in his and didn't need to say anything as they sat holding hands through the tears.

'Mum, you can't go back to the flat. I've come to take you home with me,' Rhys said, trying to sound confident and in control, but feeling very unsure of the response he might receive.

'Have you now,' was all she said, as they held each other's hands.

Chapter Eleven

The following day, after some deft negotiation, Rhys left the hospital with his mother to set off for Liverpool.

The hospital authorities were satisfied that Bronwen was fit enough to be discharged and were both pleased and relieved that she had somewhere to go. Rhys and his mother had managed to set aside any further difficult conversations and she had agreed that, in the circumstances, a return to the flat was neither realistic nor safe. She had accepted her son's offer and agreed to go with him to stay at his house in Liverpool, albeit with reservations, at least for now.

***

Glyn returned to the flat a few days later and was surprised not to get an answer when he knocked at the door. He had left the kitchen window unlocked as a precaution so went around to the back of the block and climbed onto the flat roof to be able to access the flat through the window.

He stood in the kitchen for a while listening before opening the door into the hallway. No one was at home. Glyn looked around the flat and could see that someone had been in and he remembered that someone was there the night he left. *Who would that have been?* he wondered. It was also evident to Glyn that things were missing. Not many things, but the sort of things you might take if you didn't plan to come back: photographs, a toothbrush, a few clothes, papers. *Why would that be? She's gone*, he concluded. But why and where to?

Glyn thought back to the night that he had last seen her. A bit of a slapping, he remembered, but no more than usual, so why had she gone? He felt uneasy. Was anyone else involved? *Whose tongue has been wagging?* he asked himself.

Glyn let himself out through the front door and paused

to look around before knocking on the door opposite. *That nosey bitch will know something.*

The door opened slowly and just enough to look out.

'Oh, it's you. You're back again then?' said the lady occupant.

'Obviously. Where is she?' he asked gruffly.

'She's gone. Best thing, if you ask me,' she said as she tried to shut the door, but Glyn caught it before it closed tight.

'I was asking you, bitch, where the fuck is she?' Glyn shouted, forcing the door further open.

Frightened, the lady threatened to call the police as he laughed.

'They wouldn't want to come here, love. Too much trouble. Now, are you going to tell me here or shall I come in?' he said, threateningly.

***

So, someone sent her to hospital.

He ran down the stairs, leaving the poor woman terrified on her own door step. *That must be Tremodog*, he thought, *but that was days ago. Will she still be there?* he thought. *No, she's probably not.*

Glyn googled the hospital number on his phone and called. After a while, he got through to reception to ask about his 'wife'.

'She's been discharged, sir,' he was informed.

'Oh, thank you,' he replied politely. 'Where to, please?'

'A private address, sir.'

'Oh yes, of course,' replied Glyn, lying but trying to sound convincing. 'Which one was that?'

'In Liverpool, sir.'

'I see, thank you.'

Well, well he told himself. The return of the prodigal son!

Glyn felt like a drink and walked towards the main

street in the town and the pub. He walked past the usual town landmarks and picked up a pie at the butchers on the way.

He ordered a pint and looked around the bar as eyes were turned towards him. He sensed that he was less than welcome, although that was a feeling that he was used to.

'What are you staring at, Mr Williams?' he asked, recognising the old one-time shopkeeper.

'Glyn Morgan, what brings you here?' he replied.

'None of your business, can't a man just have a pint in peace?'

'I wish you could, but seeing you usually means trouble. What do you want this time?' asked Mr Williams.

'That's nice, isn't it?' Glyn replied, turning to face his audience.

Inadvertently, one of the other regulars let slip that Rhys had been in the pub recently.

'That's interesting,' Glyn replied. 'What was that spineless little shit doing back here, away from his fancy new world in Liverpool, or where ever he is?'

Silence fell and Glyn cast his eye across the room. 'Oh, I see. He came looking for his mum, did he? And you nosey bastards told him where she was living, I suppose?' he paused. 'Am I right?' he demanded, looking hard at all those in the bar.

Nothing was said but the inference was clear. Glyn finished his pint and left, angrily muttering to himself.

So it must have been Rhys who disturbed me in the flat, he thought to himself.

'Oh dear. Well, I did try to warn Rhys,' Mr Williams said. 'This doesn't bode well.'

***

Rhys received another letter from Elis asking what had happened about their mother. Rhys wrote back and explained all that had transpired and wondered how Elis would react.

Within days, Rhys received a further letter containing a visiting order and asking Rhys to visit him in prison urgently. Rhys felt that he had no choice. He booked the visit for the first available slot.

On the day in question, Rhys was feeling a little under pressure, trying to maintain things at work and adjust to accommodating his mother. However, he did feel that he and his mother were getting on better than he had expected, at least on the surface. Rhys headed for the prison in the morning traffic, trying to meet the demands of his last remaining brother. Despite his determination, delays on the roads were inevitable. *What could Elis have to say?* he wondered.

After leaving his phone in the car and checking through the usual security measures, Rhys was escorted through to the visits room and allocated a table to wait for Elis to be brought across the prison to meet him. Rhys speculated how Elis might react to his news about their mother. Would he be pleased, grateful even? Would he be jealous or angry? He wasn't sure. Whichever way it was to be, however, Rhys knew that Elis would soon let him know.

Prisoners started to arrive and were being searched before being directed into the visits room one at a time. Elis was third in the queue and soon caught his eye and wasted no time in coming over to his table.

'Hi, Rhys, it's good to see you, thanks for coming!' Elis said enthusiastically as the two brothers shook hands.

'No problem, it's good to see you too. I have some news about Mum.'

Rhys explained all about the events in Porthmadog, what he had found and how he had taken their mother back to his house in Liverpool, at least for now. Elis seemed quite shocked; he evidently hadn't realised the full extent of the situation.

'So the miserable bastard took it out on her more than usual this time and she ended up in hospital?' he responded.

'Yes, I reckon that's what happened. She didn't say

much, nor was she minded to make a complaint. From what I saw, however, she must have been severely beaten and was badly bruised. After she left the flat, I expect some kind soul took pity on her and called an ambulance,' replied Rhys.

'Complaint. Complain to who, Rhys?' challenged Elis, obviously starting to get angry.

'Well, the police, I suppose.'

'Do me a favour, Rhys. What good would that do? They've done nothing all these years!' said Elis bitterly.

'OK, Elis, you're right. Anyway, calm down or you'll attract attention from the guard,' counselled Rhys.

Elis quizzed Rhys for details about the flat and what he had found. He wanted to be aware of all that was known that linked Glyn to the incident.

'I thought about trying to confront him, Elis, but what's the point? Mum's safe now.'

'But is she? How long will you keep her with you? And what makes you think that Glyn won't find you?' posed Elis.

'That's interesting. One of the locals said that too, that Glyn wouldn't just let her go but would find us both. Then what?'

'Come on, Rhys, have you gone soft with your slick city life? You know what he's like. You know what he's capable of.'

'Yes, I suppose so,' said Rhys quietly.

'There is no "suppose so" with Glyn, you know that,' replied Elis unequivocally. 'Listen, I've been thinking, and I have a plan. We can't just leave him or Mum will never be safe again.'

'What do you mean, Elis?'

'I mean I want him dead, Rhys, for all that he's done. If I was out, I'd do it myself, but I'm not. I can arrange it, though,' said Elis quietly and calmly.

'How can you do that?' responded Rhys indignantly.

'Rhys, I live with murderers, gangsters, racketeers, fraudsters and drug dealers all the time. I can call in a favour, Rhys. I can easily get two heavies to sort him out, to help him along his way and make it look like suicide, then there'll be no investigation.'

'But how would you know what they'd done, Elis? How could you trust them?' asked Rhys.

'Simple, Rhys... because you'll be there to witness it and then you'll tell me.'

Rhys sat back in horror.

'No, Elis, I can't say that. He doesn't deserve it, and I've left all that behind. I can't get involved in something like this!'

'Careful, remember the staff are watching. Just try to look calm, laugh a little, look relaxed,' Elis warned.

'Relaxed!' Rhys responded. 'You've just asked me to murder my own father!'

'No, Rhys, you don't have to get your hands dirty, just ensure for us both that it happened.'

'It's not that simple, Elis. If I'm there, I'm complicit. Under the law, I'd be as guilty as the heavies. You must have heard of joint enterprise?'

'It won't come to that, Rhys. Trust me. He'll be found by some innocent hanging sometime later and assumed to have killed himself. The police will be happy to see the back of him and so will the local community. There'll be no enthusiasm or need for an investigation. It will be recorded as suicide,' Elis tried to reassure him.

Rhys went quiet.

'Rhys, this is important. It's Mum's safety we are talking about here, and yours. It's family loyalty, Rhys. He deserves it, you know that, and they won't be able to touch us for it.'

Rhys remained quiet for a moment.

'How will you fund it, Elis?'

'I'll sort out the details. Paying two heavies is no problem. I'll just ask one of the drug dealers in here. A few thousand is nothing to them,' said Elis, conscious of the time.

'OK, Elis, but I'm only a witness, no more, alright?'

'OK,' Elis concluded, looking at his watch.

A bell rang and the visits session was about to be brought to an end. The two brothers loudly exchanged their goodbyes and a few last minute messages from family.

'I'll let you know about that date, Rhys,' Elis said as he was led away and Rhys was left to wonder what the hell he had agreed to.

Chapter Twelve

Glyn had agreed to meet two guys in a disused factory in an industrial estate out of town. It was quiet and he felt confident that they would be undisturbed. He was due to be paid off for his part in a stolen car racket linked to a second-hand car dealership. Talk to the right people and cars could be stolen to order, documents forged, cars transformed and put back on the road.

Glyn was looking forward to getting his money. He had his own debts to pay after all, feeding those further down the criminal supply chain. *Then*, he thought, *I can go and find that spineless son of mine and his pathetic mother and show them who's boss*.

It was a quiet evening, just about dusk, when Glyn arrived at the designated location on foot. He stood in the old building, not sure what it had been used for in a former life but that didn't matter. It was all about his money.

He heard a car draw up and, shortly after, two men appeared. He didn't recognise either of them. *That's strange*, he thought. Once the men had approached him and spoke in Eastern European accents, his suspicions were aroused, but it was too late by then.

Glyn was trussed up carefully, a rope placed around his neck, and then he was dropped from some height from a metal girder inside the old factory; it was all designed to ensure his demise. The men were careful. They left no trace. They had done it before.

The men had been told to expect Rhys to arrive just after them.

'OK, mate, you can go in now. He's dead. His neck is broken. Just be careful. Don't touch anything,' said one of the men, glancing at Rhys as they calmly left the building. They got back into their car and headed off back down south.

Rhys approached the hanging body cautiously. Yes, it was Glyn Morgan, no doubt, and yes, he didn't need any medical training to know that he was dead. It was a strange moment after all these years. Years of abuse and regret to end like this, but Rhys felt some relief that this was another important milestone in his life. Once he was sure that he could confirm to Elis what had happened, he turned and left.

Rhys walked out of the old factory building. He checked that no one was around and returned towards the footpath running through the area. He removed his plastic shoe covers and walked away along the path, leaving in the opposite direction. He didn't want to be seen or associated with the area at all. He had booked a place on the last train out of town, not back to Liverpool direct but to Shrewsbury, where he had parked his car. He wore a long jacket and a hat and felt confident that no one would know or recognise him at the station or on the train. He sat alone throughout the journey. No one checked his ticket. He had paid cash.

Two days later, three work men clearing the site for redevelopment sensed an odd smell and, on investigation, found a hanging body. The emergency services were called and the body was pronounced dead. It was a male later identified as Glyn Morgan.

The police's initial investigation could find no indication of foul play and concluded that Mr Morgan had taken his own life.

The senior investigating officer held a meeting to wrap up the case.

'So, Glyn Morgan had finally had enough.'

'No one will regret his passing then, gov?' said a colleague.

'No quite,' the SIO replied.

'Are you totally satisfied that it was suicide then, boss?' asked another.

'No. You can never be totally sure. I can think of a long list of people who would happily see the demise of our Mr Morgan, but there was no forensic evidence that would satisfy a court and, of course, no witnesses. We could conduct an investigation, but I guarantee that it wouldn't lead anywhere. I haven't got the resources so we will let this one go.'

'Do you think someone did him in then, boss?'

'Probably, but I can't prove it. It could well have been suicide, God knows he had plenty to regret and feel guilty about.'

'A professional job then?'

'Could have been. Not guys from round here. We'll never know for sure. Anyway, I hope that signals an end to the torment of poor Bronwen Howell, after all these years. From what the hospital told us, any more beatings like the last one and she would be lucky to survive.'

'Natural justice then, gov?'

'You could say that, but it's not for us to make such judgements. Just keep your ears to the ground, see if any of the local snouts can tell us anything, or if any of the local players seem to have gained from it. We could always reopen the case, if necessary.'

'It was suicide then, boss?'

'Yes, it was suicide.'

PART TWO

Chapter Thirteen

Late summer 2017

Rory had promised to call in on the Zukas family on a Wednesday evening and was conscious that he had postponed the visit several times already, so he felt that tonight he really had to go. By the time he left the office he'd had enough really, but he was determined to follow through on the commitment he'd already made.

When he arrived at the house, only Mrs Zukas was at home and she greeted him like a long lost relative. She invited him inside, insisted that he had coffee and homemade cake while she unloaded all her anxieties about her son.

'You see, Mr Scott, he is basically a good boy. We work hard, and so does he, and he studies for his exams. He wants to be an electrician, you see.'

She continued to tell Rory how well her son was doing.

'So what's the problem, Mrs Zukas?' he asked gently.

'Oh, it's the other boys – they are jealous. They don't want to see a foreign boy do well or get on. We don't like it, but we can take a bit of that. I get it too, shouts across the street, abuse in the supermarket. I've even been spat at, but for Matis it is different. He is third generation, he sees himself as British and doesn't understand their attitude and he resents it. He's a young man, they goad him and I worry that he will react, like he did before, but next time it could be more serious. He's boiling inside, I can tell. A mother knows.'

'OK, I see, and how does he see it?' Rory asked.

'He doesn't say much, but I think he shares the same concern.'

'OK. I'll ask him – will they be long?' Rory enquired.

'No. Matis and his father should be here anytime now.'

'Is it specific people who goad him, Mrs Zukas, or is it more general?'

'I suppose it's both actually. One or two are the worst, but he does get it from all sides.'

'I wish I had my magic wand with me, but there isn't an easy solution here. People harbour their prejudices and that isn't going to change easily. He must learn to deal with it without losing control and, if he does retaliate, not to go over the top,' said Rory, trying to be both realistic and helpful.

'Oh you are so right, Mr Scott, and we tell him the same. Maybe if he heard it from you that would be different,' Mrs Zukas suggested.

The phone rang and Mrs Zukas intimated that it was Matis calling as a passenger from his dad's van. He suggested that they would be late, another hour at least, so Mrs Zukas passed the phone over to Rory for him to talk directly. It gave Rory an opportunity to repeat and reinforce the message that he had already suggested to Mat's mother. He got the impression that Mat understood but was not confident that he would be able to comply. *Time will tell*, thought Rory as he tried to reassure Mrs Zukas.

'Tell him, if he really feels on the edge, he should ring me and I'll attempt to talk him down. OK?' said Rory, conscious that this represented a fairly clear signal of an increase in risk.

'Thank you, Mr Scott. You are so kind,' she replied.

'We try,' he answered.

***

Back in the office the following day, Rory recorded his concerns about Matis. Together with the police intelligence information, he was aware of Matis's involvement in potential disorder and violence was in fact much more serious than it appeared. Rory managed to book an appointment to see Stacy Browning, who by now had been transferred to HMP Drake Hall in Eccleshall. He would visit the following week.

Afterwards, he had to complete breach papers to arrange for the recall of one of his offenders on licence and therefore a return to prison. There was a little more flexibility with breach these days, Rory considered, but this guy had basically not complied and so there was no doubt in his mind that breach was the appropriate course of action. He knew he couldn't afford to take too many chances with high risk cases.

He was covering office duty for the rest of the day, in the absence of a colleague who had left and still not been replaced. The delay in appointing staff was deliberate in order to save money, he considered. *In fact, they may well never be replaced at all*.

***

The following week, Rory set off to visit Stacy Browning at Drake Hall. She was now three months into her sentence and it was time to liaise with the prison probation staff about her sentence plan and to start to consider likely release arrangements. Three years didn't seem long for taking a life, but killing someone with a car had always been an anomaly and somehow seen differently than causing death by any other means, he reminded himself.

For the poor mother of the victim, it was obviously devastating. Rory was well aware of that from regularly reading harrowing accounts of the impact on those affected by serious crime, but dealing directly with victims was not his role; he was tasked with dealing with the offender, in the hope of reducing the risk of harm to the public in the future. The impact on this particular offender was substantial too: the loss of her job, maybe her career; the loss of reputation; and the loss of a relationship. She would also lose her rented apartment. In other words, her life had been completely disrupted too, but she was the driver, she was the adult and it was she who had lost control of her car and mounted the pavement.

However, the death caused was not premeditated so, in

a sense, it was accidental, as the driver she had no control over who might be heading towards her on the pavement at that time. In the final analysis in the eyes of the law, however, she was solely responsible.

When Rory met her, the impact of this experience was palpable. Stacy Browning was drawn, had lost a considerable amount of weight and was very subdued. She spoke quietly and softly. She expressed her appreciation for him visiting but didn't really engage beyond the superficial. Rory did not judge that his visit had been a waste of time, just that he was disappointed that it obviously wasn't going to be more focused. She was not ready to discuss the offence in any detail or consider her future at this stage. She was still in a state of shock and was struggling to accept and adapt to her change of circumstances. He felt worried about her and shared his concerns with the duty prison staff, who noted his observations and promised to keep a close eye on her. He asked if she had received any other visitors, which apparently she had not.

'What's been the reaction of the other prisoners?' he asked.

'Hostile, as you'd expect. Death of a child is always emotive and prisoners feel added resentment when they perceive that one of the toffs, so to speak, has joined their number. She's a lawyer too; they expect her to know better.'

'I see,' replied Rory. 'Is she in danger from the other prisoners then?'

'Yes, but we have to deal with that all the time,' the officer said calmly.

Rory felt uneasy as he left the prison – the phrase Penny Patel had used came back to him: the prison was like a cauldron of emotion, always on the boil. He felt that he knew what she meant; he could feel it in the atmosphere in the visits room.

By the time he arrived back home, Rory was feeling emotionally drained. The job took its toll, he knew that, and this was one of those moments. He felt fortunate to come home to his family on days like this. Emma had become attuned to his reactions and was very good at understanding how it might feel. She would give him space when he needed it and not pry or try to interrogate him.

Chapter Fourteen

Elis opened a letter from Rhys and sat quietly in his cell, eager to hear any news. Rhys told him that their arrangements had all worked well and that Mum was OK, although she would need some time to recover and adjust.

That was all he needed to hear. One of the other prisoners from Wales had told him that the suicide of Glyn Morgan had been reported in the local press so that, together with the news from Rhys, had confirmed in his mind that they had seen the last of Glyn Morgan.

It was a rare occasion that Elis actually felt proud of his brother and even, dare he say it, almost close to him. No, they were quite distant really, but there was still some bond nevertheless. Elis hoped that, in time, Rhys would be able to visit him in prison and bring their mum along too. He felt that he now had something to live for. Maybe it was time to change his attitude and cooperate a little more with the authorities and even aim to work towards a potential release... Was it a vain hope? *Probably*, he thought, but he still felt that it was not totally impossible.

The local police had visited Rhys at home to formally confirm the loss of his father. *A very odd moment*, Rhys thought as he tried his best to feign surprise. When they left, the two officers were relieved.

'Well, that went better than expected, didn't it?'

'Yes, very much so. They say it's one of the most difficult parts of the job, having to deliver the news of the death of a family member, but he didn't seem very surprised or even that bothered, did he?'

'No, mate. It takes all sorts!'

The Senior Investigating Officer overseeing police involvement in the death of Glyn Morgan had reviewed all available information again. His team had reported nothing of any significance from their local snouts or any whispers in the community. He looked at the forensic report again and there were no fingerprints on the body or the rope. The report did mention the presence of various footprints in the dust on the factory floor but there were many and the impact of wind and rain through the decaying building made it impossible to discern how old or recent they might be, or whether there were any real patterns to the footprints.

He concluded that nothing had changed and that he had made the right decision. He recorded his findings and closed the file.

***

Bronwen was starting to feel a little better and was trying to adjust to all that had happened in the last few weeks. Her bruising was subsiding and, fortunately, there were no further indications of any broken bones. Underneath her frail appearance she was really quite a tough and resilient person. She had needed to be over the years, to protect the children if nothing else.

She felt real ambivalence about the death of Glyn. She knew nothing of the involvement of her two sons, of course, but as regards the loss of her 'husband', well, he was never much good at fulfilling that role. Still, whilst he was violent and unreliable, there remained a glimmer of affection for the man who had been in her life the longest. Not that she would miss the beatings or even the area where she grew up. No, she thought this was a chance for a fresh start where nobody knew her or would judge her based on her past, or at least that was what she hoped for.

She didn't even miss a drink. It had been tough for those first few days in the hospital, but she had been through withdrawal many times before and had learned to cope with it. Maybe this time she was ready to try to give it up all together. Maybe she wouldn't need it any more, now that Glyn had gone and she had a clean and decent place to stay. *How long might that last?* she wondered, but did not dare ask.

For his part, Rhys was getting to quite like the company

of another person around the house. In a strange sort of way, he felt that this gave him a chance to recover and experience some of the elements of family life that he always felt so bitter about being denied. Despite having broken away from his family and having moved into academic life, Rhys found that he actually felt a real connection to this woman. The woman he had vaguely been aware of and that he had called mum for all these years. They actually were able to hold meaningful conversations and he felt that he wanted the arrangement to continue, that he didn't want it to end.

Chapter Fifteen

Emma was sure that Poppy was growing every day! The constant changes and developments in her baby were a real revelation to her. She was surprised about how much she was enjoying the experience. Yes, she obviously felt tired and did, to some extent, miss the stimulation of going to work, but the closeness to her own child, the experience of breastfeeding and watching her grow, were all very different but intrinsically valuable experiences in their own right.

Her fledgling business was also growing steadily. Whilst working from home, Emma was careful in managing her time between the demands of family and business. Her old contacts had been good to her in passing work her way. Whilst she knew that wouldn't last forever, she was grateful for the help in launching her new venture. She was currently working with a medium-sized technology firm who provided innovation and advice to some of the leading firms in computer and mobile phone development. She was helping them to plan and position themselves for a successful expansion programme. Part of what she offered was simply trying to instil the confidence to expand and to concentrate on the opportunities and not over-emphasise the risks.

Emma also felt more comfortable about living in the village although she still had a hankering for something more. She felt that there was scope to take what they had learnt from the experience of buying The Old School House and apply it somewhere else, somewhere with more choice over the community that they lived in. She had been thinking about this for a while now and was starting to formulate some more concrete ideas. She had been discussing it with Michaela, who she had met in the village, and agreed that it sounded like a really good idea. In fact, she felt sure that her husband, Pat, would agree with her and want to live in such a place too!

***

All seemed to be going so well when Emma received some bad news. Her mother had been found dead at home by a neighbour. Nothing other than natural causes were suspected, but it was so sudden and an awful shock. *Poor Mum and poor Poppy*, thought Emma; *her only grandparent and to lose her so soon.*

After all the upset of the loss of her mother and the responsibility of the funeral, Emma had talked to Rory about having a holiday before summer turned to autumn. They both felt like they needed a break. They favoured something modest with Poppy at this stage, so a UK-based self-catering holiday seemed like the best option. Emma agreed to research holiday cottages not too far away, somewhere by the sea. *Wales perhaps*, she thought.

While Poppy was playing in her cot and watching Bracken's every move, Emma was searching on her computer and found several really nice places on Anglesey off the North Wales coast. Rory had agreed to let Emma book what she thought was the most appropriate option for the second week in September.

She settled on a two-bedroom cottage near Red Wharf Bay, on the east coast of the island – a place with ready access to walks on the beach. There was also a well-known pub there called The Ship Inn that had a good reputation. Emma felt excited; they had not been away for a while and this would be their first family holiday with Poppy. She would be just over three months old by then, not ready for walking on the beach or swimming in the sea but at least she could experience some fresh air and, if it was warm enough, be able to dangle her toes in the sand and the shallow rock pools.

***

Rory managed to fit in a visit to Stafford prison. He was required to attend an oral hearing with the Parole Board to consider the future sentence management of David Thomlinson, a rapist he was supervising. The man was a bouncer in a night club and had been convicted of raping several young women, who he had detained in the club on the pretext of helping them find lost property. He was serving a life sentence. The man was only eight years into his sentence with a tariff of twelve years so he would not be eligible for consideration for release at this stage, but he could be recommended for a move to open conditions.

Rory had reservations about his level of progress and his suitability for Category D status and open conditions. His report to the hearing had voiced those concerns. The offence was part of a pattern of abusive behaviour that had gone on for a long time and his underlying beliefs and attitudes had not been sufficiently challenged at this point, Rory felt.

Other bouncers had been complicit in the scam and would direct any enquiries about lost property from young women to him and then cover for him while he took them to one side. Sometimes Thomlinson would select certain young women in the club and arrange for one of the other bouncers to try to steal her phone or some other property to start the abusive process that would end with a victim, usually well intoxicated, being trapped in a small room with a big and powerful man who would not release them without having sex first.

Thomlinson had completed SOTP, the established sex offender programme before the authorities withdrew it as the standard treatment approach. Concern had been growing for some time that offenders had learnt the desired responses from the course and could readily seek advice from other sex offenders on how best to 'play the game' and get through the programme with a good report that would help them progress through their sentence. Rory acknowledged that making judgments about how genuine offenders were in any expressions of regret, remorse or insight into their offending was always difficult and could not be entirely scientific – it would be, at the end of the day, only a professional opinion.

Rory was concerned that, despite David Thomlinson's protestations of insight and a change of attitude to women in general, there were still intelligence reports coming from the prison about female staff feeling uncomfortable in his presence and of an unhealthy fixation with certain female officers.

Rory presented his findings, he hoped in a balanced way, but recommended further work before any re-categorisation. Thomlinson and his lawyer vigorously opposed Rory's suggestion, knowing that any decision not to approve open conditions would necessarily mean a delay of another two years before a further opportunity to convince a hearing would be offered.

Presentations and reports followed from various prison staff, including his offender supervisor and psychologists working in the programmes department. When the Parole Board conclusions were released, they stated that David Thomlinson would need to provide clear evidence of a change in attitude, reflected in his day to day behaviour, and undertake more work in regard to education and vocational training, before there could be any further consideration for category D status.

After the hearing Rory had an opportunity for a brief word with Thomlinson before he was escorted back to his cell. He was feeling disappointed with the way the hearing had gone and was threatening to ask for a change of probation officer.

'He wasn't very happy with you,' the escorting prison officer reported back to Rory after returning Thomlinson to the wing.

'It goes with the territory, I'm afraid,' said Rory, shrugging his shoulders.

'No, you don't expect to be popular in this job!' replied the officer.

Despite the background of public reservations and the constant political criticism, Rory considered he was only doing his job and had presented a balanced and reasonable picture. He felt content that was all he could do.

Whilst in the prison, he quickly took the opportunity to visit his seconded colleagues to get a broader picture of what it might be like working in the prison. He came away feeling reassured and more determined to request a transfer. The establishment was not in the best state by any means but the opportunity was now and Rory had no influence over the state of the prisons. The building was old and tired, staff numbers had been cut over successive years and morale was generally low. However, the situation was no better in his current role and he considered that he needed a change. Penny commented to him as she took him back to the gate that staff had said how well he had conducted himself at the hearing and how that would do his request for a transfer no harm.

Rory felt pleased as he headed for home wondering what conclusion Emma had come to about the family holiday.

Chapter Sixteen

While Rhys was at work, Bron was starting to feel like she had enough energy to be useful around the house. She did a little cleaning and one night prepared a meal for when Rhys came home. He was very pleased as he was not used to this kind of service. As her bruising went down, Bron became stronger. She was eating better and looking after herself more effectively than when she was on her own and constantly in fear of Glyn's possible return.

She did make it as far as the row of local shops one morning and couldn't resist the opportunity to buy a small bottle of gin. Not that she felt an overriding urge, more the need for a sense of security that it was there if she felt that she needed it.

Sometimes, when Rhys came home, she would be prostrate on the sofa and he knew that she had been drinking. Still, he didn't challenge her, he just tolerated it.

Rhys had been in touch with the council in Wales for his mum and made arrangements to settle her arrears and end the tenancy agreement. He had agreed to pay a fee to clear and clean the property, as he knew there was nothing there worth salvaging. She hadn't even mentioned the flat and didn't want to ask the difficult questions about any future arrangements.

One evening Rhys broached the subject.

'How are you feeling now, Mum?' he asked.

'OK. I'm OK, son,' she replied, unconvincingly.

'Mum, are you happy staying here?' he asked, hesitantly.

'Do you mean you want to throw me out?' she replied, becoming tearful.

'No, no, Mum. Don't cry. I have no intention of rejecting you, having found you after all these years. No, believe me, I want you to stay. I want you here with me.'

'Do you really, Rhys?' she replied, wiping her eyes. 'I don't know what to believe anymore...'

'I mean it, Mum. We can make this work. I owe you this. It's my turn to protect you. It's my turn to look after you.'

'So, I can stay?' she said, still not really believing that this turn of good fortune could possibly apply to her.

'Yes, Mum, you can stay. This is your home too now.'

'But what about the flat, Rhys?' she asked, suddenly feeling a mild sense of panic.

'It's OK, Mum. I've sorted it. I've released you from the tenancy agreement.'

'But there'll be arrears, Rhys. The council won't let that go, and it will need to be cleared; they won't take it back in the state it's in!' she cried, starting to feel very insecure and anxious.

'It's OK. I've sorted all that too, Mum. Arrears are paid, the council will clean the flat and you don't need to worry about a thing.'

'But I'll need to pay you rent for here then, Rhys?'

'No, Mum, I don't need it. I was paying for all this on my own. I can afford to keep you too. You don't add much to the costs after all!' he said, almost with a sense of affection.

'Oh, Rhys, I don't know what to say.'

'Then just say "yes". Trust me.'

She smiled and hoped that she could.

***

Rory felt satisfied that applying for the post in the prison was the right thing to do. Laura endorsed his application and they waited to hear from the organisation. It was a part-time post and, in any event, Rory was the only applicant. After a brief confirmatory interview at the prison, both the Governor and the probation service were pleased to appoint him. Rory was excited and immediately started to tidy up his caseload at Upper Lowbridge, ready to hand over to his successor in due course. A few short meetings with the prison team counted as a handover and

Rory felt ready to start his new job, following his brief period of leave. He hoped that it would present him with a new challenge and help him to clarify his thoughts about where his future lay. In the meantime, it opened up the possibility of moving on from the community pub role that he had started and enjoyed so much, to look for something similar that was maybe more permanent.

The short break in Anglesey in the September 2017 turned out to be just the right time between jobs for Rory. He had been pleased with Emma's choice of arrangements in a cottage at Red Wharf Bay. They both felt excited too as they packed up the car ready to set off for Wales. They managed to cram in all the necessary equipment that was required to sustain a young child and felt grateful that at least a high chair and a cot were available in the cottage.

Poppy looked a little uncertain as she watched her fledgling mum and dad try to ensure that they had taken all that they would need for the week. She had experienced some journeys but not for too long, so this would also be part of her new learning experience. Emma had ensured that spare clothes and wipes were readily at hand, as well as the inevitable nappy changing kit. Bracken observed with interest, eager to ensure that a space was left for him in the car. Emma was happy to let Rory drive the first part of the journey as she concentrated her efforts on minding Poppy.

Emma was also a competent map reader. After years of travel, she was used to the process and to finding her way at home and abroad in a variety of hired cars. She had planned the route and made sure Rory knew where he was going. She had decided to take the M54 from the Wolverhampton Road leading to the A5 and mid-Wales. The sat nav was set as a backup, giving them confidence that they would find their way.

They stopped briefly near Llangollen to have a quick look at the famous canal aqueduct as it crossed the valley high above the ground. It was an impressive sight. Poppy could be fed and changed while they stretched their legs and checked the next stage of the route. They had allowed plenty of time to stop along the way, depending on how Poppy reacted to the journey. Fortunately, the weather was good and the forecast for the coming week was encouraging.

It wasn't long after setting off again that Poppy was sick, necessitating another stop before Corwen, when a convenient layby offered sanctuary and a spectacular view across the valley. Emma was taken by surprise; Poppy had not been sick in the car before. It made an awful mess and smelled vile but Poppy didn't seem too concerned as Emma did her best to wipe her down and get her back in the car seat. They set off again, with windows wide open, towards Betws-y-coed and onwards to Capel Curig.

As they felt ready for a break, Rory was looking for a convenient place where they could stop when The Moel Siabod Cafe appeared on the horizon. It looked like an old petrol station, which in fact it was, but had been tastefully converted into a spacious and welcoming cafe. The hosts were very friendly and everyone admired Poppy whilst Rory tried to look knowledgeable standing over the large map display of the local area. Emma felt like a snack and ordered what turned out to be the biggest cream scone she thought she'd ever seen! With Rory's help, they did just manage to devour it together, assisted by a pot of Earl Grey tea.

Once restored, and with Poppy's needs addressed, they headed off along the A5, past mount Snowdon and down to Llanberis before driving over one of the two bridges crossing the Menai Straits and onto Anglesey.

Emma spotted the sign to their destination along the A5025, as it meandered through the pleasant countryside. A sharp turn off the main road led to a lane down to the sea. The instructions from Menai Cottages were good and they had no problem finding the cottage just off the lane and a very short distance from the sea. Poppy woke at that moment and started to cry as they unloaded the car and found their way around the cottage. However, once inside,

Poppy started to settle and it was time for a feed.

The weather was warm and sunny, so it seemed like a good opportunity to explore the lane down to the beach. They set off with Poppy in her baby back carrier and with all the necessary equipment. They could see the pub on the right and a little restaurant as they took the path left and down onto the sand. The sea was a long way out.

'You can walk right round the cove to Benllech, the next place along the coast, Rory,' announced Emma with confidence.

'OK, we'd better keep an eye on the tide though, Em,' responded Rory, feeling protective.

'Yes, OK, but it looks a very long way out yet, Rory,' she replied.

The sand was soft under their feet and the sea breeze refreshing as they looked out to the horizon and enjoyed the freedom of the open space. There were a variety of people on the beach, from families to dog walkers and nature lovers. As they approached the edge of the bay, they could see the new holiday development on the cliff and then the view around the corner towards Benllech. Here the beach opened up to a wide expanse of sand with lots of opportunity for families to play.

They stopped for a moment and Emma laid down a beach towel and Rory extracted Poppy from her carrier. He lay her on the towel next to her mum, as Bracken adopted a protective stance, as if trying to both be useful and to remind them that he was there too! At first, Poppy looked a little bemused and didn't know quite what to make of these new surroundings. Obviously, no one had briefed her on what to expect and how to react to her enthusiastic fledgling parents, who themselves looked somewhat disappointed by her less than euphoric initial reaction to the seaside, even as Bracken chased the seagulls.

Chapter Seventeen

Later, walking back along the sand, Emma was trying to crystallise her thoughts.

'Rory, you know we've talked about our future and what direction it should take?'

'Yes, love.'

'The more I think about it, the more I'd like to try to create our own community. Our own village, if you like. Somewhere we chose and with people we chose… to build a community from scratch, based on a common outlook.'

'Um, you are feeling romantic!' responded Rory.

'No, don't dismiss it, Rory. I'm serious,' Emma replied.

'I'm sorry, love, is this tomorrow or the next day?'

'Oh, if you're just going to be like that I won't mention it again,' snapped Emma, ending the conversation.

Back at the cottage, it was time for Poppy's feed again and she needed changing, which by now was a well-practised routine between the apprentice parents.

For the remainder of the holiday, Emma and Rory were keen to maximise their time spent on the beach and avoided spending too much time in the car. They simply loved walking along Red Wharf and Benllech beaches. None of the prospective walks were too far, given the need to carry Poppy for at least some of the way and for her to avoid too much exposure to the sun. Bracken happily ran alongside them, avidly looking for opportunities to play with other dogs. Some of the beaches restricted access for dogs, even on leads. Rory was careful to keep Bracken in check and always carried an ample supply of poo bags, just in case.

Chapter Eighteen

It was several days later before Emma felt confident to raise her suggestion again in conversation whilst they were walking on the beach. Rory had been talking about how much he was looking forward to working in the prison, and how he hoped that would help sustain his enthusiasm for the job by helping to counterbalance some of the less palatable aspects of modern public service.

'I'm sure that will help, Rory, but do you still have reservations about your long-term future with probation?' asked Emma.

'Yes, of course, but for now a move to the prison is what I need,' Rory replied.

'And do you still think about the long term?' she enquired.

'Yes, I'd still like to build on my experience with the community pub and follow that up. That offers a potentially exciting new direction at some point.'

'I suppose I'm in the same position with my fledgling business.'

'Yes, something else we have in common,' Rory replied whilst turning to kiss her on the cheek.

'Rory, this is great for now, but I do want to seriously consider developing these ideas in the years to come,' floated Emma, hoping that this time Rory would share her enthusiasm.

'Yes, of course, Em. So would I...' he said, before running off towards the sea to paddle in the almost warm and very clean water.

A success, Emma hoped, as she was left standing and watched in hope that Poppy would manage to stay safely in the back carrier as she was bounced about precariously on her blissfully unaware father's shoulders.

Thankfully, Poppy was smiling and giggling as they came back towards her.

'Yes, Emma, I do want to plan for the future too. You

mentioned moving, starting a new community, so how do you envisage that working?' he asked.

'Rory, it's just an idea at this stage but, given what we've learned from the village and your role in the pub, I see a real opportunity in developing the concept. To move to an area where there is space to almost create your own village with people committed to the same ideals; to recruit a balanced and diverse community that could be sustainable and a model for a better life.'

'OK, but what would we live on?' replied Rory.

'We'd still have to work, of course. I know this can be just a romantic notion, but I'm trying to be realistic. There have been many attempts at this sort of thing but they are usually short term and based on a retrospective model – that is trying to recreate a community of old. How people lived in Viking times or pre-Industrial Revolution, for example. I'm not thinking of that, or some form of a survival exercise. This would be a modern community but incorporating many of the values and aspects of a healthy and meaningful existence that many feel that the modern world has left behind. We could still do some work as we are doing now; you on a community project, me with my own business, but lead a simpler, greener life that is more sustainable and not so dependent on consumption,' said Emma, starting to feel energised.

'Yes, OK, and not too fanciful to last the test of time,' added Rory.

'Yes, exactly,' responded Emma promptly.

Emma and Rory continued to develop their ideas during the remainder of their holiday. They visited the National Trust house and gardens at Plas Newydd and the pretty village of Moelfre but continued to spend most of their time on the nearest beaches at Red Wharf Bay and Benllech.

They patronised The Ship Inn one lunch time when Poppy obligingly fell asleep at the right time, giving them the opportunity to eat a relatively peaceful meal outside. Most of the time, however, they enjoyed their dinner in the evenings in the cottage once Poppy had gone to bed. A quiet evening, a nice meal and some music was a real treat.

Chapter Nineteen

The following day, whilst walking on Newborough beach, again Emma paused.

'Where's that, Rory?' enquired Emma as she stared out to sea at a small island situated just off shore.

'I'm not sure, Em. I'll look on the map when we get back to the car,' Rory replied.

Emma was clearly captivated by the island; it felt inviting, it felt right. Emma was instantly convinced that was the sort of place where she wanted to settle. That was the type of place where she wanted to create their own community. It looked simply perfect!

After more paddling in the shallows, Emma and Rory walked back along the sand and approached the large car park area. Poppy was getting fractious and wanted to get out of the back carrier. She was clearly uncomfortable. As Rory lifted her out, the cause of her discomfort was immediately evident as he observed a very full and overflowing nappy.

Emma was quick to rescue the situation and to deploy the changing bag, fortunately with the use of the large flat surface of an available picnic table. Rory went to find more wipes from the car and to collect the map. He handed Emma the wipes and quickly looked up the relevant page to be able to identify the mystery island that had so attracted Emma's attention.

'Here it is, Em,' Rory announced confidently. 'Ynys Craig/Rocky Island. Approximately two miles off shore and around ten miles long by five miles wide.'

'Can you sail out to see it?' Emma immediately enquired.

'I don't know, Em. Surely it's possible, but whether there's a ferry we'll have to find out.'

'I wonder who owns it. What's its history?'

Emma was obviously keen to learn everything about it and was no doubt determined to find out.

As she looked around for a bin to deposit Poppy's nappy, a Forestry Commission warden was walking past.

'Hi, can you tell me anything about the island off shore from the beach? It looks so beautiful,' enquired Emma.

'Yes, Rocky Island. You're right – it's a lovely island, a mixed history though,' replied the warden, as Emma felt pleased that she had obviously asked the right person!

'It was inhabited by a Christian community until the 1950s, by which time the population was unsustainable and the last few people were evacuated. Like most of this area, it's now owned and managed by a combination of the Forestry Commission and National Resources Wales. I'm not sure what plans, if any, they might have for the island.'

'Oh that's interesting. So it was a lively community at one time?' asked Emma, intrigued.

'Well, lively indeed. Odd folks they were. There were all kinds of rumours about strange practices on the island, apparently,' replied the warden, authoritatively.

Chapter Twenty

Emma and Rory drove back to Beaumaris from Newborough, keen to explore the possibility of sailing out to the island. Beaumaris, with its modern dock, offered regular boat trips running out to Puffin Island, albeit in the opposite direction. Emma approached the first cabin promoting such trips to enquire about Rocky Island.

'Hi, I see you run boat trips. Do you sail out to Rocky Island too?'

'Oh no, not routinely. Our service goes around Puffin Island. It's popular with the tourists, you see, to photograph the bird colony.'

'Oh, I understand, but would you run a trip to Rocky Island, or is there anyone else who does so from here?' asked Emma, hopefully.

The lady obviously wasn't keen. 'Not really, there isn't the demand for that and there's very little there to see. It's not as spectacular as Puffin Island.'

OK, thought Emma as she looked around the harbour, *I'm asking the wrong person. Maybe a small fishing boat is a better bet*, she wondered.

Walking back towards Rory, Emma felt inclined to go and ask a few of the locals. 'What did she say, love?' asked Rory.

'No luck there, but one of the locals might ferry us across. I'm going to ask,' responded Emma.

Um, she's determined to visit this place, thought Rory.

Emma approached a gentleman in a small craft who looked like a well-weathered and experience fisherman.

'Hi, we've spent the morning on Newborough beach and seen the island just offshore and fancy going to have a look. Is there anyone here who might be prepared to ferry us across, do you know?'

'Um, there might be,' reflected the old fisherman. 'What's your interest?'

'I understand that there was a lively community there

once?'

'Who told you that?' enquired the fisherman defensively.

'I spoke to one of the wardens on the beach. You see, I'm interested in islands and, ultimately, in the possibility of forming a new community somewhere, so an island location is appealing.'

'Well, I don't know about that. You can't just go and live where you like.'

'No, I appreciate that, but I'm exploring the idea. Anyway, we'd like to see the island. Can you take us?' asked Emma.

'It's not quite that simple, you see. The tides are very strong around here – the island can be difficult to get too. That's one of the reasons why it was eventually abandoned. We would probably be able to get close, though, but not necessarily land there. It's private, anyway, and I don't think the owners welcome visitors.'

'OK, but can we try?'

'You are determined, dear, aren't you?' replied the old fisherman kindly.

***

After feeding and changing Poppy again, she was ready for a sleep. Rory and Emma enjoyed an ice cream while deciding what to do.

'I don't think it's sensible to take Poppy on the sea, so one of us will need to stay here with her while the other goes to the island.'

'Yes, OK,' replied Rory. 'Well, as Poppy has been fed and is asleep and it's your idea, do you want to go and I'll stay here with her?'

'I could do – I'm used to small boats. My dad often took us on trips on family holidays. OK, let's do that,' confirmed Emma.

Confidently, Emma walked down the beach towards the old fisherman who, by now was ready to set sail. She felt reassured that his boat looked safe and he looked more than competent.

'Come on then, young lady. Jump aboard and let's see if we can satisfy your curiosity. As I said, though, I can't guarantee that I can land. You might only get a view from a distance.'

With that, Emma nodded and they set off along the Menia Strait, with the benefit of the tide, and set off out to sea.

Rory felt a little apprehensive, but he could see that Emma really wanted to do this. *So why not?* he thought.

The boat picked up speed and moved efficiently through the waves. The sea was calm and the weather was warm and sunny with clear views along the coast and beyond. The fisherman knew the water well and guided the boat using the best of the current, so they very quickly emerged from the straits and cruised near to the coast in line with the island. As they approached, Emma could see the derelict remains of several buildings and what looked like fields that had previously been prepared for pasture. There were rocks around the shore of the island so, as the old fisherman had warned, landing was not guaranteed.

He competently sailed around the island sufficiently far away from the rocks to be safe.

'Look, there is what's left of the old harbour and landing point, but it's in a poor state of repair, best leave it alone.' Emma agreed, thinking of Poppy and not wanting to take too many risks or to take too long. She had seen what she wanted. On the face of it, the island was a viable place to rebuild a community.

Chapter Twenty-One

As their holiday drew to an end, they felt ready for home. It had been a lovely time and they had been so lucky with the weather, which had stayed fine for most of the week.

As Rory drove back Emma took the opportunity to catch up on some sleep and awoke just before Rory pulled into the car park at the Tyn-Y-Coed pub in Capel Curig for a bite to eat. The pub car park featured an old stagecoach as a reminder of its past as an important inn on the long route from London to Hollyhead and across to Ireland. Emma fed Poppy and changed her in the car first whilst Rory took the opportunity to check the oil and water, which were both fine.

The pub was actually quite busy but there were other families too and people were tolerant of a degree of noise and disruption inherent in having children. They enjoyed eating a sandwich and a few chips between them. *What a nice pub, well worth a return visit*, they thought. As they headed for home, Emma remained fascinated by the island and looked forward to finding out more.

***

Back at work the next day, Rory was feeling even more under pressure. There had been a short delay in his move to the prison. Caseloads in the community team were rising with no prospect of any replacement, let alone additional staff for the foreseeable future. Senior managers, for the most part it seemed, had bought into the macho business-like culture that repeated the mantra that this was how it was and you were expected to deal with it. Rory felt that they continued to expect total adherence to all the standards and processes in order to protect the organisation but showed little concern for their own staff.

Newly allocated cases were appearing on his caseload almost daily, it seemed, without the proper opportunity to assimilate them. Most were of course complex, high risk and in immediate need of attention. *The expectations are becoming ever more unrealistic*, he thought.

All this was in addition to trying to consolidate his work in preparation for the move to the prison, where he hoped that working part time would prove to be easier to manage.

Rory had just received two cases of life sentence prisoners coming towards the end of their sentence and having secured potential release arrangements to Staffordshire hostels. Such cases ideally should not be transferred so close to release, necessitating the building of new working relationships at such a critical time, but the reality was somewhat different.

Both men had some family connections to the county, although they had been living in different parts of the country, and had been supervised by other areas so far throughout their sentences. Rory anticipated a reasonable chance of a successful transition from open conditions to living in a hostel, which he considered actually was not that different, but the challenges would emerge in placing these men in the community later on in their licence period.

Rory tried to get on and concentrate on finishing several key tasks before the end of the day.

An hour later, reception asked if he could possibly see someone who had finished their licence period but was in need of help. Somewhat reluctantly, as he accepted that he was the only officer available, Rory agreed to see the man.

A quick look at his file revealed that he was a long-standing offender and had been associated with the probation service over many years. Michael Roach had last been supervised in the West Midlands and had connections with both Birmingham and Coventry. Previously, he had lived in Staffordshire, around the centre of the county, for several years before Rory had joined the service. It appeared from what Rory could glean that dishonesty, alcohol and drug abuse, mental health issues and homelessness had been constant factors in this man's supervision.

'Hi, Michael, I'm Rory, one of the probation officers, come on in and let's see how we can help you,' Rory announced as he collected Michael from reception. He didn't appear to be drunk but was looking unwell, stressed and dishevelled.

A brief interview revealed a looming crisis with the threat of eviction, probably linked to a deteriorating state of mental health. Michael said that he had been released from prison six months ago after serving three years of a five-year sentence for robbery. Initially, he described being directed to a voluntary hostel in Coventry where things had not turned out well; he claimed to have been beaten up by another resident and left before the completion of his licence period.

'You see, gov, I came back here hoping to stay with my brother for a while, but he's got a new partner with two kids and could only offer me the sofa for a few days, but time is running out and I've already overstayed my welcome. Can you help me, gov? I need somewhere to go,' explained Michael, looking more and more vulnerable.

Oh dear, thought Rory, *I can't hand out instant solutions in these circumstances*. He would need to check out what he was being told, his status and any liability for breach of licence or recall to prison. All of which he knew would take time and time that he didn't have.

'OK, Michael, I understand but I don't have a magic wand. You'll have to give me a while to make some enquires. Can you come back in an hour, please?'

Michael nodded and duly shuffled out of the office, saying that he would return as instructed.

Rory quickly started to make some enquires and a disturbing picture emerged. It was clear that Michael Roach had not been assaulted at the hostel in Coventry but that it was he who had assaulted another resident and had absconded soon afterwards. A warrant was out for his arrest and a return to prison looked inevitable. The assault had been serious and further charges were pending. Enquiries indicated a pattern of non-compliance, a long history of offending and a very poor discipline record. Finding this man accommodation in the community would be difficult enough, especially at short notice, but in all the circumstances an arrest would secure both his own safety and that of the public whilst providing accommodation, albeit not what he was hoping for.

Rory rang the police and told them of his findings and concerns. Whilst they understood the situation, Michael Roach was not going to be a priority given the current state of police resources. Should Michael return to the office as instructed, Rory wondered whether any other members of his large family could provide him with a bed in the short term, whilst the police looked to arrest him, or of course they could intercept him at the office.

In the event, Michael failed to return as agreed and, having reported the matter to the police, Rory continued dealing with his other priorities, trying to complete several urgent matters before the end of his part time week.

In the meantime, Michael Roach had jumped onto a train to Birmingham in the hope of securing a bed at the Salvation Army hostel or the night shelter.

Chapter Twenty-Two

Bronwen was starting to feel more confident and wondered whether it was the right time to move back to North Wales where she felt that she belonged. Rhys had been kind but was staying with him really a long-term option?

By the afternoon, she had decided to leave and had rung Megan and secured an offer of a place to stay for a while. Bron packed her few humble possessions and decided that it was best not to share her plans with Rhys in advance, but to just leave. She left a brief note thanking him for his help and informing him of her plans before walking the relatively short distance to the railway station. Leaving Liverpool behind, she boarded a train to Porthmadog. She expected to arrive at Megan's that evening, and she was looking forward to seeing her again.

When returning home from work Rhys noticed a police check point and suddenly felt really anxious as an officer pulled him over. He immediately thought of the events relating to Glyn's death but tried to stay calm. In the event, the officer was enquiring whether any drivers had seen anything relating to a major road accident around the same time the previous day. Rhys felt so relieved but tried not to show it. On balance had he done the right thing or just allowed himself to be pushed into his part in his father's death by Elis? He could never be a hundred percent sure, but reconciled himself to having to live with the uncertainty and the guilt. By the time he got home he felt more confident that he had made the right decision but was disappointed to find that in the meantime his mother had left. On reflection however he was not surprised. He felt pleased that she had benefited from her short stay, that when it mattered, he had been able to help her, and she at least left with a thank you and a forwarding address. More than he deserved, possibly. Now he could be sure that Glyn presented no threat to her, perhaps it was for the best.

Moving away, and breaking from the past, had been a significant step for him and maybe a step too far for his mother. Anyway, that decision was hers to make and she'd made her choice. He felt that he could live with that. He just hoped that things worked out for her.

***

Staffordshire police had no success in securing the arrest of Michael Roach, so the warrant remained unserved. It wasn't until several days later that the significance of that fact became apparent.

The evening television news reported that a known offender with a significant record of violence had been arrested in connection with a murder in Birmingham city centre in the early hours of the morning. A business man on his way to the airport had been accosted at a taxi rank by a Michael Roach who demanded money. After the business man refused his request, he became aggressive and, after a short altercation, stabbed the man several times in the chest, resulting in his death.

And then the enquiry started...

Questions were raised in parliament about the role of the statutory agencies, the effectiveness of supervision and the risk to the public, resulting in the tragic death of an innocent passer-by.

The police mounted a robust defence of their failure to execute the arrest warrant, arguing that recent levels of severe cut backs and the consequent loss of officers left significant gaps in their capacity to protect the public.

The national probation service referred to their duty to hold a serious case review, following which they would seek to learn lessons from any failures identified.

Discussions in Staffordshire soon reached the initial view that this case had all the hallmarks of the usual conclusions of such enquires; the failure to record, to transfer information and confirm realistic arrangements for handover of supervision requirements between areas were all likely to be identified as critical factors in the lead up to the murder of the business man, who was later named as Rashid Patel.

In fairness, Laura and Rory both felt that criminal justice records, including those of the probation service, were actually quite thorough compared with many other agencies, and the sharing, availability and transfer of information between areas was usually good. It transpired, however, that Michael Roach was still subject to licence from his last prison sentence when the murder occurred, so there was a gap in information from Coventry that could have assisted Rory when he was faced with seeing Roach, especially given that Roach had not been entirely honest in presenting his circumstances. The receptionist was adamant, however, that he had claimed to have completed his licence and was therefore effectively seeking help as an ex-offender. Given reduced resource levels, many services would in fact have refused to see him, if they believed that they had no statutory responsibility. Chasing up arrest warrants for breach of licence or supervision was an old point of contention. Delays often caused problems and it was not uncommon for offenders to effectively 'disappear' for extended periods of time, which was clearly unsatisfactory.

As the enquiries got underway, Rory found that he was drawn into the process. It wasn't long before two key questions emerged and he was asked to account for his actions. Was the information available on the record system that Michael Roach was subject to statutory supervision when Rory saw him? Should he have contacted the police straight away with a view to facilitating an arrest forthwith?

Rory inevitably felt bruised by the process. He had agreed to see a man presenting as in need when, strictly speaking, it was not even his responsibility; he was not the duty officer that day. In checking the records, time was limited and, from a quick scan, he felt that what was immediately available, albeit sketchy, was sufficient information to feel confident in seeing him. Thereafter, he felt his actions were measured and reasonable.

It became apparent that information was recorded by Coventry staff in regards to the assault committed by Michael Roach and that records did show that he had absconded, while still subject to licence, and that a warrant had been issued for his arrest. Questions emerged, however, about appropriate flagging up of such risk factors and the ability of an officer to access the most pertinent summary of information quickly.

As regards facilitating his arrest, Rory felt that, by informing the police, he had done what was expected of him and, although he sympathised that they were not able to respond immediately, that was clearly not his responsibility.

Unfortunately, coverage in the press was not so guarded and balanced as suggestions continued to be made that Rory had been negligent in his duty. He was criticised for his failure to research all the information available to him and, in doing so, he had failed to protect the public as a first priority. The press deemed that he was therefore, at least in some part, responsible for the subsequent opportunity afforded Michael Roach to murder Rashid Patel.

The experience was very public, humiliating and hurtful and did nothing to enhance his sense of loyalty and commitment to the organisation. On the contrary, it only served to hasten Rory's desire to look beyond the service and move on at some point. After the serious case review and the internal enquiry were concluded, Rory was pleased that, whilst some criticism remained regarding his actions, he was not held ultimately responsible and that his move to the prison, having already been agreed, was allowed to continue with the full support of both the prison and the probation services.

Chapter Twenty-Three

The holiday soon felt like a distant memory as Rory started his first day in his new job at the prison. After all the pressure of his last job, and the enquiry following the death of Rashid Patel, Rory couldn't help but view the prison as a potential sanctuary for a while. Some of the implications from the enquiry would rumble on for a while yet, he considered, but at least he would have a break from it.

Despite still feeling harshly criticised, Rory did have to accept that a man had died and, however imperfect the criminal justice system was, that yes in a sense it had failed Rashid Patel and his family. It was a sombre thought. *Did I do enough?* he wondered in his darker moments. *Indeed, would it ever be enough?* In the end, Rory felt that he had to take some solace in believing that he had done what he could, nevertheless Rashid Patel had still died. He had been killed by the offender Michael Roach, not him, he reminded himself, but he would have to live with it. With no formal disciplinary action to follow, his only choice, he recognised, was to decide whether or not to stay in the probation service. At this point he felt unsure, but he was continuing to question if that was appropriate.

His new colleagues at the prison tried to be supportive and understanding about how he must be feeling but they had their own pressures too and there was work to be done. Rory completed his basic induction, including key security, a tour of the prison, a brief talk from the governor and a more detailed induction from his new line manager. The prison was in transition, with primacy for case management transferring back to probation officers and the return of a full-time probation manager with each prison-based team. For the probation officers, it was a welcome development, but for some of the prison officers who had been covering that area of work, and in fairness doing a good job, this felt like a regrettable step backwards.

The team was expanding as Rory arrived to replace one of the members, with two extra officers and the new manager arriving all at about the same time. The new manager had worked in prisons before and had the necessary previous experience of working with sex offenders. Stafford Prison being a specialist establishment dealing with that particular type of offender.

Rory was familiar with OASyS, the same offender assessment tool that he had used in the community, and he found the prison computer system easy to adapt to and operate. Carrying keys, locking gates, and being much more security conscious all became relatively second nature fairly quickly, he found. It took a while to be confident in finding his way around the prison, although it was a relatively small site. Learning names was a challenge – with all the colleagues from a variety of backgrounds and, of course, all the new prisoners. By and large, the initial contact with prisoners was mostly positive, although David Tomlinson was not entirely pleased to see Rory in his new role.

The work did seem to be more concentrated and specialised. Processing the expected volume of work, however, was still demanding, especially at the start of a secondment. Report writing, sentence planning, attending oral hearings with the Parole Board and risk assessments of various kinds he found were the main features of his work.

Rory was allocated a caseload of prisoners to supervise and needed to become familiar with their circumstances promptly. Two cases required immediate attention so he started reading up their files before arranging to meet them. The first case was Daniel McIntyre, serving fifteen years for rape. He had a current and a previous conviction for committing stranger rapes – attacking young women at railway stations. His attacks involved threats and use of violence to subdue his victims before dragging them into dark and secluded places to rape them. Victims were invariably traumatised as well as physically brutalised.

His level of cooperation throughout his sentence was not consistent and questions remained about his level of understanding, acceptance of responsibility and remorse. He had recently completed a suitable course, specifically designed for sex offenders, and Rory had an invite to his post programme review, which was to summarise his response to the course, identify any further work and plan for the remainder of his sentence. His probation officer from his home area would also be in attendance – this was standard practice to maintain contact with the home service in advance of release and resettlement. Rory had, of course, attended such reviews previously in the role of the home officer. Now he needed to switch his attention to acting in the role of the seconded probation officer, working in the prison.

The second case was John Sidmouth, serving ten years for the rape of his partner. He was waiting for a Parole Board oral hearing to determine his suitability for a move to Category D open conditions prior to release. Rory would need to assess all the relevant information and write a report for the hearing, either supporting such a move or expressing reservations. John Sidmouth had completed work identified for him in his sentence plan, together with some basic education and vocational training. From the file read, Rory's initial impression was to support the application for open conditions.

***

Rory met Daniel McIntyre briefly before the post-programme review and was able to reassure him and gain some more insight into how he was thinking. The review was chaired by Calum Marshal, Rory's new senior probation officer and line manager, on Calum's first day in his new role in the prison. Rory was impressed by how well he handled it. The report outlined progress made, recognising the positives and was realistic about identifying the deficiencies, the gaps and the need for further work. Daniel was encouraged to take the comments on board and express his own assessment of his progress on the course. His outside probation officer from the home area felt that Daniel's performance was encouraging but acknowledged the need for further work.

After the review, Rory had an opportunity to approach his new manager.

'Hi, Calum, I thought that went well!'

'Yes, it did. No doubt you've attended many such reviews?' Calum replied.

'No, actually I only started here last week. Like you, I'm new here too!' Rory responded.

This was to prove to be one of several new introductions as the reformed probation team took shape. Rory was aware that, over recent years, probation resources (in line with most public services) had been subject to severe cuts in funding and therefore in staffing levels. The team was to be restored to an SPO and four officers for the first time in many years.

At their first team meeting, Calum was able to confirm some basic team roles and functions and outline how he saw scope for development over the next few years. Jakub Donurski provided the continuity as the experienced member of the team and Ann-Marie Popescu, Becky Jones, Rick Stanley and Rory were the new officers. Rick and Rory were both working part-time. Although there was much to learn and challenges ahead, there was at least a note of cautious optimism within the team.

Chapter Twenty-Four

Emma continued to build her confidence as a mother and, although she found motherhood hard work, she was enjoying her time with Poppy and the challenge of trying to balance that part of her life and her business interests.

The new parents were amazed at how quickly Poppy grew and developed with seemingly some new advance almost daily. Late autumn announced the arrival of winter as the family experienced their first Christmas together. Christmas 2017 proved to be a fairly quiet affair that year with all their different responsibilities. Poppy was a little more responsive but they recognised that her most enjoyable Christmases were yet to come.

Rory regained some confidence after the enquiry and its aftermath and restored some enthusiasm for his job. He found prison work to be intense, but rewarding and less chaotic than dealing with offenders in the community. His work at the community pub was rewarding and he felt that he was achieving steady progress with some key ideas.

Emma made some enquires about the island she had seen off the Anglesey coast. It transpired, as she had been led to believe, that the owners had no plans to sell or use the island and that, realistically, therefore there was no prospect of pursuing that as an option for their project. Nevertheless, a further idea had been planted.

Chapter Twenty-Five

Emma and Rory had identified some useful contacts to help explore and direct their ideas about a model of future living. Several environmental organisations were keen to help support the idea and several sources of potential funding had been identified. The biggest obstacle, however, remained finding a suitable site.

The essential break, the spark of luck, came early in the new year of 2018. One of the environmental groups she had been in touch with informed Emma that an opportunity had arisen to buy another island, called Ynys Hebogau (Island of Hawks). It was a little further down the coast where they had been looking before, off Newborough beach and just past the spit of land that housed some old fisherman's cottages and a disused lifeboat station. Emma immediately tried to ring Rory in the prison but couldn't reach him, so had to satisfy herself with informing Poppy instead, who failed to show the same level of interest. *What a prospect*, she thought, as ideas flashed through her mind!

Registering a bid and raising the necessary funds would be the first obstacles to overcome, she thought. She felt reasonably optimistic about attracting funding from various sources and, of course, there was a sizeable inheritance from her mother's estate. Emma wondered what her parents would have thought about the prospect, or indeed the opportunity to potentially part-fund the venture. She really didn't know how they might have perceived the idea.

Once Poppy had gone to bed that night, Emma and Rory sat up into the small hours. They talked about the island opportunity and started planning their response. Having visited the first island, Emma was confident that this second location would be similar. Both wanted to visit the area again but felt instinctively that this was the chance that they had been looking for and that it was too good to miss. If they were to be successful, however, they appreciated that they would need to move quickly. Rory could spare some time whilst meeting his commitments to the community pub over the next few days to start things going. The first thing was to confirm the legitimacy of the sale and to register an interest. They would need to appoint a solicitor and hoped that one of the environmental groups might provide that service. Then they would need to secure sufficient funds relatively quickly to have any realistic chance of completing a purchase. All sorts of possibilities ran through their minds about approaches to fund raising and shared ownership, but they would be later considerations, they appreciated.

Rising early the following morning, Rory made a start on implementing some of the approaches that they had decided the previous evening. By coffee time midmorning, Rory had secured agreement in principal to the legal services of one of the groups and outline offers of funding, or at least not immediate refusal, from several others. They were still some way short of raising the asking price of two million pounds, but it was a good start.

Emma had followed up the advert to find out more information about this alternative island. Apparently, it was significantly bigger than Rocky Island and had the advantage of being accessible by foot at low tide on most days. That would make it far more viable and provide a potential balance between accessibility and seclusion. The island was described as approximately twenty miles long and five miles wide at its widest point. There were some existing drivable tracks, some old buildings and extensive wild life, including seals, otters and various birds, although it had been some time since any hawks were reported to be on the island. The highest point was over four hundred feet. It was privately owned and had been occupied at various times in the past, with the last residents leaving in the 1960s when the owner planned to build a hotel and leisure complex on the island, although that never materialised. It had only been used occasionally since then by different wildlife and conservation groups. Emma couldn't find anything to suggest any established local interest in buying the island, although she realised that may change.

Over the following few days more progress was made and, using maps and Google Earth, a more thorough impression of the island emerged. Some of the buildings appeared to have the potential for restoration or conservation. Some of the land showed signs of previous cultivation and the limited network of tracks looked to be usable. The solicitor had started making some enquires about what level of services might already exist on the island, particularly water and electricity, and whether planning permission seemed likely to be granted.

As the New Year progressed Emma and Rory's expression of interest had been acknowledged and financial support was looking a little more secure. The couple continued to look forward and to plan accordingly, anticipating that even if successful the purchasing process would still take several months. Even then it could be quite some time before the island would be ready for habitation and they could sell The Old School House with confidence, adding a potential boost to their funds. Over the forthcoming twelve to eighteen months, Rory anticipated that the pub community project could well become self-sufficient and that his role would come to an end. If that proved to be right, then he would need to secure alternative employment if their aspirations were to be fulfilled.

It was time to turn their attention to recruiting some fellow residents to join the project. They felt that Emma was probably better suited to heading up that particular task and she started to work out a viable approach. Their research in relation to funding had already attracted some limited interest in the possibility of joining the project as part of a new community on the island. Emma started to consider whom she would need to target to create a viable and sustainable community.

Included in her first draft list were the following: a doctor or nurse, a farmer, a teacher, several naturalists/ornithologists, people with general outdoor living/country skills, some people with trade/building skills, a couple of competent sailors, maybe even a priest... They would probably also need a mechanic, some business people to generate income, a shop keeper and an expert in green power to develop wind, wave and solar energy. *There, not a bad list,* she thought. Whilst generally looking for couples and young families, some diversity in the group by gender, race and ethnicity would also be preferable.

How would they go about the recruitment and selection of such people? And how many people would they need, both initially and over time? What would be the expectation of their financial commitment? There were clearly going to be many issues to be worked through and resolved.

Chapter Twenty-Six

Rory was preparing for his first Oral Hearing before the Parole Board as a prison-based probation officer. He had interviewed John Sidmouth and explained why he would not be supporting his application for a progressive move to open conditions yet. The degree of progress suggested in the various reports and on file wasn't reflected in the responses Rory extracted from John face-to-face. He seemed to have regressed and was not very forthcoming. Also, there had been a very recent positive drugs test, indicating that he had relapsed into using drugs in the prison. Drug abuse was a significant risk factor identified in his offending and, as such, any return to drug use had to be of concern. Rory accepted that the job obviously involved giving people messages they didn't want to hear, but he found that most offenders accepted that reality if you put it to them straight. They generally didn't take well to waffle or to what they perceived as 'bullshit'.

In any event, the hearing was relatively straight forward after John's solicitor had persuaded him that, considering all the circumstances, applying for open conditions was not going to be successful and his best approach would simply be to acknowledge that and lay the foundations for a more realistic application at the next hearing.

The Parole Board members recognised from the solicitor's address that such a conversation had probably taken place and gave John credit for his realistic approach, concluding that further work and progress were both necessary and achievable by the time of the next hearing.

Whilst this wasn't what John Sidmouth hoped for, Rory could work on the Parole Board's advice and it reflected how the whole process could be constructive in changing offender's attitudes and assist in rehabilitation. John would also need to demonstrate commitment to resisting the ever-present drug culture in the prison and to provide a series of negative drugs tests to demonstrate that he was clean.

By now Rory had made himself familiar with most of his other new cases and was arranging to see them in turn. Several OASyS reviews and assessments were due and the full range of other reports related to risk. Rory was enjoying the new challenge and the more relaxed, less intense attitude of most prison officers, alongside their robust sense of humour. Dealing exclusively with sex offenders was different to what he had been used to but, generally, he found them to be less confrontational than other offenders. They could be devious and hard to move forward but, on the surface at least, they were often quite compliant.

Emma's business portfolio was growing and the feedback she was receiving from clients was encouraging. She was enjoying the independence and the flexibility that it afforded. Balancing her endeavours with the needs of a young child was inevitably demanding but she felt that, for the most part, she was coping. She wasn't able to devote as much time as she would have liked to planning for their future, but she recognised that any transition to a new life would be a long-term project. Most of all, she was happy with the direction her life was taking and recognised her relative good fortune.

It was evident one morning that Poppy was not having a good day and was unsettled before Rory was due to take her to nursery. After Rory had left with a disgruntled child, the post arrived. Emma was trying to catch up and started opening letters whilst attempting to empty the dishwasher.

A letter from a lecturer at Liverpool University was interesting, offering to conduct some research relating to their project.

When Rory returned from work having collected a much more settled Poppy from the nursery, he found Emma looking tired. *Maybe Emma wasn't dealing with the multiple demands on her time as well as I had expected*, he thought. Rory had become used to responding immediately on return home and carried on dealing with Poppy while Emma tried to regain her composure. Poppy was happy to sit on the floor and play with Bracken, whilst Rory tried to console Emma. The following couple of hours were the usual whirl of attending to Poppy. Feeding, changing and bathing ensued, interspersed with brief dog walking before peace resumed at bed time and Emma and Rory could start to exchange the news of the day and think about making some dinner. Cooking had become less of a pleasure and more functional with the regular use of a few staple simple and quick recipes. Tonight was to be no exception. They prepared the meal together and ate one at a time whilst needing to settle Poppy who was a little fractious.

When Rory eventually sat down, he picked up one of the environmental publications they had been reading that expressed support in researching the project.

'Oh yes,' Emma remembered. 'Our advert inviting initial enquires about joining the project features in that magazine you are reading, Rory, and there's a letter somewhere from Liverpool University offering to conduct some research.'

Rory found the advert and read it with interest whilst Emma searched for where she had left the letter from earlier in the day. Eventually, Rory found that he was sitting on it and started to straighten it out to be able to read it. Emma noticed a puzzled then surprised look on his face as recognition dawned.

'Em, this is from Rhys Howell, one of the Howell brothers who I supervised briefly on licence and transfer from North Wales. He was a bright lad trying hard to break away from a criminal background and evidently went on to complete his education and now works as an academic! It's him who has written this letter offering the services of the University to research, monitor, and evaluate the project – that's great news!'

'Is he reliable?' asked Emma.

'Well, I assume so as he's made it to that position. He's been quite influential in academic circles. He's more into social policy than our particular angle, but he is offering the services of a range of academic staff. Em, this is a useful opportunity, we must run with it,' Rory responded enthusiastically.

Rory did write back to Rhys accepting his kind offer to conduct some research on their behalf. He hoped that this would prove to be a useful addition to the project.

Rory found that the demands of the community pub were becoming more manageable and so he had more time to concentrate on the island project. Several individuals and couples had already shown an interest and applications were starting to arrive in response to their advertising. Rory was encouraged by the apparent quality and diversity of the applications.

Emma had been working on forming a project management group who could help steer their course. Their solicitor had confirmed that basic services – water, sewerage and electricity – were already established on the island and that he had received favourable indications in response to his application for outline planning. Purchase negotiations were also in hand but, it was far from guaranteed given the level of interest from other parties. Emma had successfully managed to recruit several able people with financial, business and environmental expertise to join the management group.

After reviewing the applications to join the project and live on the island, Emma and Rory were considering how best to make their selection. Finance would be a limiting factor that, unless they could secure sponsorship, each applicant would need substantial funds to access a share in the project. An initial paper sift reduced the applicants to a workable number and the management group were planning to invite people to an event, including a presentation, interviews and some team exercises, to help tease out both compatibility and suitability.

The whole management group was also planning a visit to the island to confirm their outline plans and to seek reassurance about several questions that had arisen.

Chapter Twenty-Seven

February 2018

The New Year heralded an opportunity to return to Anglesey and to visit Hawk Island. Following some debate, it had been decided that it would be best to appoint an independent chair to head up the management group. Emma and Rory didn't want to lose control of the project but recognised the limitations of their expertise and availability to complete the task effectively. Of the members of the group, Sir David Young was the obvious choice as a recognised financier and business man who also had a keen interest in community and environmental issues. He was prepared to accept the challenge and had the full support of all the members.

Tasks had been allotted before the group walked across the sand at low tide towards the island. After two full days of investigation on a range of issues, they were ready to share their preliminary conclusions. Emma and Rory had taken the opportunity to explore and to dream.

'Rory, I really love this place,' said Emma. 'It just feels right.' Then she leaned forward to kiss him.

Rory responded warmly and agreed that this was where he wanted to be too. This was where he wanted to raise their children. This would be a tremendous experience and achievement, if they could just secure the purchase of the island.

Back on the mainland, the main conclusions reached were:
1. The project was feasible and the asking price was reasonable.
2. The island had capacity to grow to support up to a hundred people.
3. Their initial planning on identifying the necessary skills required within the group was sound.

4. Some of the buildings were suitable for restoration and renovation.
5. There was scope for some cultivation and both arable and livestock farming.
6. Initial recruitment seemed likely to identify a viable starting group.
7. Further finance would be needed at all stages – for the initial purchase of the island, to complete its development and to generate a sustainable model.

Sir David was keen to build a hotel on the island to attract business and tourism and to consider the need for a drivable causeway across to the island, similar to that crossing to Lindisfarne off the Northumberland coast. The group also agreed to accept the offer from Liverpool University to work with the project. Attention then moved to the selection of the candidates.

***

When the time came, eighty candidates remained to compete for fifty places. Not all were available to attend but seventy people presented themselves for the event.

The presentation outlined the concept, the geography, the financial implications and the uncertainties and unknowns. A tour of the island and some informal interaction preceded the interviews. The management group were impressed by the commitment and enthusiasm of the candidates. Selection became relatively straightforward, with the likelihood of final availability and finance dictating the allocation of places as much as perceived suitability. All this, of course, was dependent on the success of their bid to purchase the island in the first place. This was made very clear to people from the onset, although the commitment to the principles would remain and the search would continue for a suitable site if in the end Hawk Island could not be secured.

The participants all seemed to have given the venture

serious thought and bought into the concept of a self-supporting community. They also seemed to be realistic and not too romantic about the need to generate sustainability; they saw that the project could not be some green fantasy but instead a well-grounded enterprise.

The team exercises identified those who could work collectively and accept the responsibility inherent in an independent and self-supporting community. As well as skills already identified, several applicants were also artists, writers, bird watchers and fishermen. Some also had craft experience, ranging from making their own clothes to wood carving, pottery and weaving. The variety and depth of knowledge and experience was really heartening. As Emma and Rory engaged freely with the candidates, they were really encouraged by the warmth and rapport within the group, which was evident from the beginning.

PART THREE

Chapter Twenty-Eight

March 2018

There was great excitement in the Old School House as the news came through that their bid to purchase the island had been successful! News soon spread across the village, bringing phone calls, messages and callers to offer their congratulations.

Michaela and Pat were the first to visit to share their delight as one of the couples in the village who were earmarked to join the project. Sir David sent a text message from the management group. All the various phone signals excited Poppy and utterly confused Bracken, who appeared to wonder what was happening. On his morning walk, everyone congratulated him and his master as he looked up as if he just accepted the accolades regardless. Rory couldn't believe the reaction of the locals. *Are they that keen to get rid of me?* he wondered for a moment before concluding that no, they were genuinely pleased for him and Emma.

The uncertainty had remained right to the eleventh hour, with Sir David able to bring influence to bear and to secure the necessary investment to meet the asking price. It was clear that the decision to appoint him as chair of the management group had been a wise move. His personal standing and reputation had been vital in gaining additional financial support. Sir David was conscious that he would need to explain the composition of the final financial package to Emma and Rory, knowing that it represented a compromise. Raising all the necessary funds exclusively from the participants and would-be residents he realised was always likely to prove to be a difficult, if not unobtainable, aspiration. The external financial support that he had now secured would assist in the launch of the project. Nevertheless, he felt, it did not invalidate the ambition of ultimately establishing an owner-occupied, self-governing community, in a similar way to the arrangements that had been secured on some of the Scottish islands.

Although Poppy was too young to understand, Emma still talked to her about it. When she tried to explain about moving to a new home on the island they had all visited recently, it was as if Poppy seemed to accept it without concern. They all laughed and could imagine that if she was a little older she might suddenly appear with her coat on and a small bag of vital personal possessions, including her favourite teddy, and announce that she was ready to go to the island!

'Oh, it's so exciting, Rory. I can't wait to see how Poppy responds to a new life,' said Emma sympathetically.

'Yes, I'm sure she and Bracken will cope with it all,' remarked Rory as the dog appeared with wagging tail to share the moment.

After the initial euphoria had settled down, Emma and Rory had to consider their next steps. Nothing was going to happen quickly, they realised. Sir David had advised them that it would be sensible to seek the joining fee of £10,000 per prospective resident at this stage, to test commitment, as well as boost the funds. *This would be a good use of some of some of the money from my inheritance from Mum's estate*, thought Emma. Rory had been very quiet all through the recent adjustment to the loss of their mum and was no doubt holding back some of his reactions. Emma thought she ought to ask him how he felt.

When the opportunity came that evening, Rory obviously found it difficult but was very clear in his own mind how he saw things.

'You see, Em, after all that has happened, I can't still regard the woman who brought us up as my mother. It matters less now that she's no longer with us, but I suppose I regard her as your mother now, not mine,' Rory tried to explain.

'Do you think about who your real parents might have

been?' asked Emma.

'No, not really. I don't know them and don't feel any strong sense that I want to at this point in my life. No, I accept what happened but struggle to forgive Mum for not telling us, but that's history now. Rather than dwell too much on the past, I'd rather look to the future with you and Poppy. You are the ones that matter to me now.'

'Ah,' responded Emma, giving him a hug. She knew he didn't like to talk too much about it so thought it best to leave it at that.

***

It was possible to begin some of the necessary works whilst planning permission was being processed. For example, checking the state of the basic services to the island, integrating power supplies with new sources of green energy and improving some of the network of tracks would be a suitable starting point, thought Emma.

Planning permission was agreed in due course for a first stage development of twenty residences, a large communal hostel, some storage/workshop capacity, a communal meeting hall, and a shop/pub/cafe/village hub near the landing station on the mainland side of the island. Some farm buildings would be renovated at the far end of the island and the initial phase of the hotel/bed and breakfast would be situated roughly in the middle between the two.

Sir David and his team had attracted sufficient funding to cover the work from a wide variety of business, government and environmental sources. His confidence in managing the project was one of the many positive contributions Sir David brought to the role. It would inevitably take some time before the residents would be ready to sell their own properties and buy new ones on the island, and even longer before any income would be generated directly from island enterprise. Another member of the management group handled media, publicity and liaison with the University research project. The local council allowed them to erect a simple display explaining and promoting the project at the car park on Newborough beach, which soon attracted significant interest.

Another group member handled social media and the writers, artists and photographers in the group could get underway recording and cataloguing events in their own way. Both local and national news media engaged with the idea and *Countryfile* was keen to feature the project on one of its programmes.

The appointed engineers made a promising start on setting up a combined wind, wave and solar power system, designed not only to service the needs of the island but to be able to sell electricity back to the grid. Bill Paterson was a retired electrical engineer who presented as the ideal candidate to take the lead on power and utilities maintenance once the contractors had finished their work. Fortunately, Bill was available to work with the contractors some of the time to learn how the system worked as it was being set up. Time invested which proved to be invaluable at a later date.

Wyn Williams, aged forty-five, and his twenty-year-old daughter, Megan, were farmers from North Wales who brought with them a wealth of local farming knowledge. They already had a plan for their transition from one site to another. Dai, Wyn's oldest son, was due to take over the farm in North Wales when his dad and his sister moved to the island. Between the family members, they were able to cover for each other and offer help and advice in setting up the island farm. Initially, they planned on reintroducing sheep to the island, together with a few pigs and chickens. The scope for arable farming was limited by the weather, felt Wyn, but he intended to persevere.

Adra Khan, aged fifty-two, from Bradford, was to head up the pub/shop/cafe. She was a woman with a big personality, lots of warmth and years of experience in retail and hospitality.

Angus Cameron, aged forty-seven, from the Isle of

Skye, had been selected to run the hotel/bed and breakfast. He had useful experience not only in the hotel trade but of island life itself. He also had an awareness of the necessary balance in attracting tourism but preserving the peaceful community existence they had all bought into. Angus kept in touch but was not likely to join the group for a while yet.

***

By late spring 2018, the project was already underway with the restoration of several buildings under early consideration. One of the larger buildings earmarked for the farm would initially be set up as a temporary shared living/hostel facility to allow some people to move in prior to individual family houses being quite ready for occupation. It could be handed over to the farm later, or possibly remain as a hostel for visitors and temporary or short-term workers.

At this point, Emma and Rory needed to make a decision. Were they prepared to take the risk to sell their home and move onto the island with their family, taking up residence in the hostel at this early stage in the development of the project?

'Rory, I think we should move. There are clear advantages in being on site as the project gets underway. We have already decided that it represents our future, so I think we should go,' declared Emma decisively.

'Yes, I agree,' responded Rory. 'There doesn't seem any point in delaying. I can wind up the handover of the community pub management fairly easily at this point. I will need to give probation three months' notice of resignation, of course, which I suppose – if we are lucky – could tie in with the sort of timescale involved in selling the house,' he speculated.

'OK. That might prove to be optimistic but let's put the house on the market. Poppy isn't in school yet, so we don't have that complication for a while. They were aware of a local primary school in Newborough, so there was local provision, although obviously in time they hoped to open a school on the island. Oh, Rory, it's so exciting!' said Emma, moving in to embrace him.

The Old School House was valued in the region of £300,000 so they put it on the market initially at £310,000. It soon generated considerable interest and, in due course, they accepted an offer for £305,000. Rory's application to leave the probation service was accepted with some sadness from both colleagues and offenders alike, but Rory felt convinced that the time was right. The probation service was moving in a direction he didn't agree with and living with that discomfort was not getting any easier. On the whole, he had enjoyed his service but was ready to move on.

Leaving the relative security of his permanent post of course represented some risk, but with Sir David's help, Rory had managed to secure funding for six months from a consortium of wildlife organisations to start a conservation project on the island. This represented an exciting new challenge and an income, at least in the short term. Emma would be able to continue her business from the island to some extent, with Rory's help, so at least some continuity could be maintained, they considered.

As the time progressed towards starting their new life, Rory, Emma and Poppy got more and more excited. The villagers wished Emma well with her plans as she continued to try to explain to Poppy what it might be like to live on an island. Their friends had been very kind and supportive during their tenure in the village and Rory felt satisfied that he was leaving the community pub both in good hands and in good order. There were inevitably those that they would miss from Coppermere but modern communication would help them to stay in touch, if they wanted to, or of course they would be welcome to visit!

Chapter Twenty-Nine

Things had moved on perhaps more rapidly than Rory had expected and it was soon time to leave the prison after only a short secondment. In some ways, Rory would have liked to have served there for a little longer, but it was not to be. He had consolidated his probation experience, learned more about offender programmes aimed at addressing the prisoner's behaviour and attitudes, and gained a greater understanding of a fellow criminal justice agency. If things failed to work out on the island, Rory knew that he could return to this type of work, but that in all likelihood this chapter of his life was at an end. He had established some good working relationships with both prisoners and staff, but it was time to hand over and say goodbye. Goodbye not only to the prison but to the probation service, for whom he had worked since leaving university and with whom he had anticipated remaining for the whole of his working life.

In the event a brief gathering, a few kind words and good wishes was all that the modern workplace could muster as he handed in his keys for the last time. Rory walked out of the prison to start a new life, which only some people seemed to understand, whilst others considered it was pure madness. He had managed to secure a short-term contract as a conservation officer but, beyond that, the future with a family to support was uncertain. *Oh well, nothing ventured nothing gained*, he considered, as he looked forward not back.

On 15th September 2018, Rory, Emma and Poppy, together with Bracken the dog, moved to start a new life on the Island of Hawks. Initially, they stayed at the hostel but it wasn't long before their house, the first of the project to be renovated, was ready for occupation. The management group had been careful to select design and building materials for the future and the new homes were innovative, very well insulated and efficient. They were built to withstand island weather to the best of available specification at the lowest possible cost. The move from Staffordshire would leave them with some excess funds from the sale of the old house, which was also helpful.

By the end of September 2018, somewhat unexpectedly, Emma found that she was pregnant again! Emma tried not to think too much about the timing, but to be philosophical. They had always wanted more children, but not just yet. She wasn't sure how she would cope with two young children. Still, it wasn't the prospect of carrying a baby but the giving birth that worried her. *That's for the future*, she kept reminding herself.

Rory was pleased to receive the news, if a little surprised too. He shared Emma's concern about coping with the new arrival so early after their move to the island, but he felt that they could manage. It was autumn, which would mean Emma would be due in the summer. *Another summer baby*, Rory thought.

The pub and community hub was the next building to be completed and Emma and Rory were delighted to welcome Adra to the island. Although there were inevitably uncomfortable aspects to living on a building site, Adra was determined to get the pub, shop and cafe up and running as soon as possible to register a good start and attempt to generate some income. There were already a steady number of visitors arriving almost daily, either to work, visit or research progress on the island, so the pub and cafe actually did quite well. It was even able to offer part-time employment to two local people, which all helped in establishing good relations. It was also a very welcome additional service for the builders and all the other workers on the island.

With Bill's help, the green alternative energy initiatives were soon ready to produce more than enough power to supply the early needs of the new settlers. Bill was so proud to be able to move into his small single house unit and call it home. In good weather at least all the existing tracks were suitable to drive on. Wyn planned to have a quad bike present on the island and would have access to tractors and other equipment as necessary, when the weather turned to winter. Wyn's daughter, Megan, moved into the new farm house as soon as the basics were established, whilst the builders were happy to work round her to finish the house. Some existing outbuildings could also be renovated and ready for use fairly quickly, and plans were in hand to erect a barn.

Before starting on the remainder of the housing due for renovation or building, the workforce looked to establish the medical centre, which could also be used for other community purposes, including at some point a nursery or indeed a school. Cat Beeston, aged twenty-five, who was to be their resident nurse, was available to move in during October, and she would soon be followed by their French couple, Marie-Clare and Jean-Paul. They were also in their early twenties and latterly from Sussex, as nursery nurse/teacher and photographer/artist respectively. Their interests overlapped to the point that, at times their roles could be interchangeable, which would add another useful dimension to the project.

One aspect that had remained undecided would also need their attention at some point. The ancient remains of an old church were still standing on the site and could potentially be rebuilt and used again in some form. Debate, such as had taken place, generated mixed feelings about the need for a religious dimension to life on the island and, if it was to be present, in what form? After further consideration, tentative approaches were made to various churches to explore the possibility of establishing a multi-faith centre. A single denomination did not seem appropriate and there was some support for a humanist approach too.

Chapter Thirty

By the end of October, the weather had deteriorated considerably. The winds were stronger and the tide was higher. Megan was starting to become concerned. When, by Friday morning, she mentioned the possibility of taking some extra precautions, the reaction she received was certainly not what she expected. The builders generally were complacent and shrugged their shoulders.

'You worry if you want to, love,' said one of the bricklayers. 'We work in anything. All year round, all weathers!'

Megan chose not to argue with him, but she remained concerned that both the weather and the forecast were really not good.

She walked across to the shop and found Adra. 'Hi, Adra, are you OK?' she enquired.

'Yes, fine. Why shouldn't I be?' she replied, sensing Megan's unease.

'It's just that the weather is getting worse and I'm wondering whether there's a storm coming in…' Megan replied.

'Oh, my dear, these islands have no doubt seen far worse than this. I'm sure we'll survive!' replied Adra.

Megan ordered a coffee and sat alone, thinking that maybe she was overreacting. She left to return to the farm to be able to ring her dad on the new landline – mobile communication being often unreliable in North Wales. Her older brother answered.

'Williams farm.'

'Oh, hi, is Dad about?' she asked, hopefully.

'No, sorry, sis. He's in the fields somewhere, chasing a lame sheep.'

'Oh, it's just that I wanted to talk to him about the weather situation,' she replied.

'Why, what's the problem?' her brother asked.

'I'm wondering whether to start tethering things down

on the island… the wind is getting terribly strong.'

'Oh, sis, don't panic. This is Wales!' he replied with bravado.

'OK, just tell Dad I called,' she replied.

'I will,' he said, both knowing that he wouldn't.

Megan felt belittled by the reaction of the builders and her brother and was tempted to think that they were right. *Adra hadn't been much better either*, she thought. As she left the phone to go and check outside again, the wind was howling and she became more determined. *No*, she thought, *I do know what I'm doing and I'm going to follow my instincts; there's a storm coming, I am sure of it*!

Megan busied herself gathering in her twenty chickens who had only just arrived on the previous day. She strapped down their pen. The house, she felt, looked secure enough and the outbuildings were just about finished. *Nothing obvious that I could do there*, she thought. She called in the cat and made sure her dog was safely in the brick shed.

The builders carried on repairing the roof of the house they were renovating.

'Hey, it's bloody cold up here!' said one of the lads.

'Wimp!' was the unsympathetic reply.

'Hey, look at those black clouds over there on the horizon,' he shouted to his mate.

'OK, so it might rain. We are in Wales. Come on, get on with it. Let's finish this section of roof then next week we will be able to move onto the next house.'

'OK,' he replied.

***

Wyn Williams came back to the farm house having sorted out his lame sheep.

'Hi, you OK, Dad?' called his son.

'Yes, I've got that sheep sorted. Hey, it's getting really cold out there – the wind's up, feels like a storm's coming in.'

'Oh, really?'

'Yes, I'd say so. I wonder how Megan's getting on at the island and how it's looking over there,' Wyn said.

'I don't know, Dad!' he replied.

'She hasn't rung at all, has she?' Wyn asked, knowing his daughter.

'No, Dad, not today,' he replied dismissively.

***

The last of the builders finished early for the weekend and were all off the island by four thirty, with the schedule of work completed up to date. Adra was due to visit a friend back in Bradford and Bill too was away for the weekend. Michaela and Pat were yet to join the project after their house sale fell through back in Coppermere.

Emma and family were all safely in their new house and enjoying what they hoped would be a peaceful evening and a quiet family weekend. Cat was planning on going out to Beaumaris that evening to see a boy she had met from the mainland. She just managed to drive off the island before the tide turned. Marie-Clare and Jean-Paul were working in the medical centre, which doubled as their new home. Music was playing and they were blissfully unaware of the wind outside.

By the time Megan was ready to go to bed to read her book, the tide was well on its way in. The island was separated from the mainland again and the wind had not subsided. It was ten o'clock. As she lay in bed she began to worry. *Will I be alright here on my own?* she wondered. By eleven o'clock, when she had not managed to go to sleep, she got up to ring her dad again.

'Williams farm, Wyn speaking,' came the familiar reply.

'Dad, it's me, Megan. I haven't disturbed you, have I?'

'No, no, love. I was just doing some accounts and thought I ought to leave it now until morning. You OK?' he asked.

'I think so, but Dad, there's a storm coming. The wind here is terrible. I wonder if I'll be alright…'

'Oh, yes, I'd noticed the wind myself. If you were worried, why didn't you ring earlier?' he asked.

'I did, Dad!' she replied. 'I told that brother of mine to tell you, but I knew he'd forget!'

'OK,' said her dad calmly. 'Well, there's not much we can do now, love. The tide will be well past the island. What exactly are you concerned about?'

'Well, will the buildings be secure? The folks here are lovely people generally but they are not used to island life. They are all a bit romantic about it. I tried to warn them, but they thought I was being silly.'

'Oh, OK,' responded her dad, recognising what his daughter was conveying to him. 'What would you want to do now if you could then, Meg?'

'Nothing really. I checked the chickens, strapped down the hut and made sure the cat and the dog are OK. I can't do much more than that, but if the weather gets worse, I fear some of the buildings, especially those half built, could be vulnerable,' Megan responded sensibly.

'Vulnerable to what?' her dad asked.

'Well, damage, I suppose.'

'Yes OK, love, I see… but the best you can do for now is sit it out. Try to get some sleep. Ring me again if you need to and we'll see what tomorrow brings, alright?'

'OK, Dad, thank you. Thanks for listening,' replied Megan, knowing that this was good advice. She went back to bed reasonably reassured.

Later, Megan awoke in the night to the sound of her dog howling in the outbuilding. As a farmer, she was used to disturbed sleep and to caring for animals in the night, so she got up without delay, dragged on her working clothes, stepped into her wellies and ventured outside to meet the storm.

The wind was raging and, despite her strapping down the chicken shed, it was lifting off the ground. Immediately concerned, Megan went to the aid of her dog

Bryn first, who was obviously distressed. He bounded out of the shed as Megan opened the door. Instinctively sensing the situation, Bryn was alert, ready to help as both of them saw the chicken shed lift, breaking the straps, and fly into the air in a whirl of feathers as terrified clucking young hens desperately tried not to be blown away in the wind.

Together Bryn and Megan guided as many of the chickens as they could into the dog's brick-built shed. Megan closed the door, knowing at least that they would be safe in there. She reckoned she'd managed to save about half of them. The rest were either being blown away or had been hurt as the shed took flight. It's too late for them now, she knew, being used to the reality of life and death in the farming industry. You can't be sentimental; they're working stock, they're not pets, her dad had taught her from a very young age. Megan led Bryn back into the house. He could sleep in her room tonight, to guard her, she thought.

Trying to get back to sleep, Megan felt uneasy. It was four o'clock in the morning. She could ring her dad again, she considered, but what was the point? She'd managed, and she had completed what needed to be done, she reasoned confidently.

By first light, parts of the island represented a site of devastation. Alongside broken half-built roofs, anything left loose was strewn everywhere and the obvious signs of a very high tide had brought in all sorts of rubbish from the sea, mostly plastic fishing debris.

Before even thinking of breakfast, Megan set off with Bryn riding on the rack of her quad bike to check on the rest of the island – having first made sure that the salvaged hens were alright. As she rode across the ground in the early morning, in places the sight that greeted her was devastating. All their work, all their effort over several months, had been reduced to debris in just one night. She was close to tears. They would recover, she knew that, but this was a warning. A reality check for the fledgling community. It was something these erstwhile (mostly) town folks had to learn, something essential about real community life – you have to help and support each other, because there is no one else.

As Megan approached the pub, she could see lights on. Adra, it would appear, was already up. She greeted Megan at the door in her fashionable dressing gown.

'No place for that now, Adra' she remarked. 'You'd be better off with a good waterproof!'

'I see,' said Adra as island life reality, not for the last time, started to dawn on her. 'Are you OK, Megan? It seems you were right, dear. I'm sorry I tried to dismiss what you said. I must remember next time. You know these conditions far better than I do,' she said, soberly.

'True,' replied Megan, feeling vindicated. 'But never mind, we need to start getting the place cleaned up. I'll check on the Scotts and the French couple. No one else is on the island this weekend, are they?' she asked.

'I've no idea, Megan. Maybe we will need to sign in and out?'

'That's not as daft as it sounds, Adra. I think we might.'

***

At the Scotts' household lights were on, and with the aid of a young child, the whole family were up and dressed early as usual. Emma responded with surprise to see Megan at her door so early.

'Good morning, Megan. I wasn't expecting to see you, are you alright?' she asked.

'Yes, I'm here to ask the same of you,' she replied.

'Oh, that's kind, but any particular reason?' Emma enquired.

'Emma, step outside and look around you.'

She did and the shock showed instantly on her face. Emma couldn't believe the degree of devastation that greeted her – the damage, the mess. Then came the disappointment, followed by a sense of anger, then finally a sense of relief.

'Oh, Megan, what a mess. Is everyone alright? What has happened here? We could have been seriously hurt!' she cried as Rory came to join her and experienced a similar reaction.

'Welcome to island life,' said Megan calmly and with authority.

***

Marie-Clare and Jean-Paul were making love as the others were chasing around the island counting heads. The children were still asleep and the household was in darkness. By the time they rose, the clean-up operation was well underway – after a full breakfast at Adra's.

'What is all this noise? What is the matter? Oh, what a mess you've made!' remarked Marie-Clare, still with the hint of a French accent, as she appeared at the café, looking immaculate at eleven o'clock, hoping for some coffee. Once the reality of the situation was explained to her, she instantly felt embarrassed, realising that the mess was not of the others' making and desperately wanted to help. Despite her fine clothes, she got stuck in with the rest of the group and helped to restore some order.

Over the course of the weekend, Sir David and the builders were informed of the situation and an initial assessment of the damage caused was completed. In short, it was a setback and not a disaster, but it might have been; they had been lucky.

The damage to the buildings would put the work schedule back by at least a month and, of course, cost money. Fortunately, the builders were willing to work some extra hours in an attempt to catch up some of the lost time. Most of the rescued hens had survived and Megan set about restocking. Egg production was important as a useful source of food on the island, and to use in the pub and the cafe. This time, however, Megan abandoned the shattered wooden hut and re-housed the chickens within the brick outbuilding in the section next to Bryn's kennel.

Clearing up the plastic debris from the sea was to become a regular feature and highlighted the difficulty of dealing with waste disposal on the island. With some reluctance, they decided that the only practical means was to incinerate any burnable rubbish centrally and take the remainder off the island themselves by tractor and trailer to the local tip. The council waste collection service was not prepared to deploy a standard heavy dust cart to drive across the sand to the island. This served to reopen discussions about a causeway to improve access to the site.

Sir David was due to visit and had suggested that they call a meeting to review progress, draw any conclusions from the experience of the recent storm, and to continue to plan for the future. When he and some of the other management group arrived on the island, they were surprised at the level of damage caused by the storm, despite Megan's ample description by email.

After he had completed a tour of the island, and had a chance to speak to all concerned, the residents gathered in the pub as Sir David had suggested. He outlined the financial position, news on publicity and media interest and said that he had some news on recruitment.

'However, let us turn our attention to the impact of the storm,' he said firmly.

'From what I've been told, and from talking to people today, the following issues emerge for me:
1. We have to adapt and learn quickly about the realities of living on an island.
2. We must trust each other and use the skills and experience within the group to their best effect—'

'Yes,' remarked Adra, interrupting him. 'You're right. I have already apologised to Megan, but we should have listened to her and we should have been better prepared.'

'Quite,' responded Sir David as Megan blushed.
3. We do need to be aware of who is in residence and who is not at any one time. Adra has offered to coordinate that

with a movements book available to all and kept here in the pub.

4. We must give some thought to an emergency evacuation plan, which raises the need for something of a harbour and access to at least one boat. We can't rely on being able to drive off in a crisis.'

Discussion readily concurred with Sir David's analysis. Rory was able to announce an update on recruitment.

'We were expecting to have twenty residents at this stage. We are in fact up to sixteen. Michaela and Pat will be joining us later once they have sold their house back in Staffordshire and Angus, who remember brings real-life island experience from his time on Skye, will be here fairly shortly to run the hotel. That just leaves one place accounting for the resident who simply failed to arrive. I haven't heard any more so assume they are no longer interested. They were dragging their feet with making the initial payment, so I suppose we shouldn't have been surprised. We are still waiting for final confirmation from another family, but there are complications. I still hope that they will be able to join us nevertheless. Ronan O'Donnell is a poet from Ireland and his partner, Betsy, is an American journalist. They have twin boys, Bradley and Luke.'

'OK, thank you, Rory. I have some further news on our last place. My old regiment have been in touch about wanting to place a soldier with us who needs some time in recovery after his recent traumatic experiences. His name is Sergeant Gary Watson, aged twenty-eight, originally from London, ex-Grenadier Guards and latterly SAS. If you agree, he would be with us for three to six months, probably prior to discharge from the army. He has received formal medical treatment but just needs some time to recuperate and, whilst we never aimed to offer "a retreat" as such, I believe that we can accommodate him. Some of his skills would be useful to us too. He has experience of small sailing craft, for example, and could coordinate an evacuation plan. If we all agree, he could join us very quickly. What do people think?'

As the group started to respond, the meeting was interrupted by a loud crash from the rear of the pub where the resident children had been playing. They had managed to collapse a display unit but, fortunately, whilst a little shocked they were all unhurt. They had managed to focus minds on what really mattered and helped bring the meeting to a conclusion.

It didn't take long before a consensus agreed to offer Gary the last place on the island and to complete the first phase of the project.

'Will he bring a boat with him?' asked Marie-Clare.

'Um, I hadn't thought of that, but actually that might be possible,' Sir David responded.

He had served briefly in the Grenadier Guards as a young officer and remained supportive of the military and sympathetic to the need to support soldiers who had made sacrifices and suffered as a consequence. The Guards had a reputation of looking after their own. A network of jobs could be made available to ex-Guardsmen in a variety of fields, but Sir David had a feeling that the island community might well suit this young man.

Chapter Thirty-One

Sir David soon confirmed arrangements with the regiment to accommodate Sgt Watson. A single house unit would be made available to him at a nominal rent for an initial three to six months, whilst he determined his longer-term plans. If he wanted to stay, then the potential was there to buy into the project. Sir David suggested direct contact and Gary soon responded.

'Hi, Sir David. It's Gary Watson from the Guards. Thank you for all you have done. I'm told I've been granted leave to stay on the island for at least three months. That sounds great!'

'Yes, you'll be welcome and, from what I've heard, this is just what you need right now. Have you any idea of the longer term at this stage?'

'No, not really, Sir.'

'It's David, Gary.'

'OK, David. None other than I've made the decision to leave the army. Perhaps I could develop something on the island – run boat trips for tourists, a scuba diving school, kayak and surf board hire, something like that, who knows?'

'Well, they are all realistic options, Gary,' responded Sir David. 'You mentioned boat trips. Has the message reached you that there's a role initially here for someone to coordinate an evacuation plan by boat and to make use of the opportunities of being at sea? Bill, one of the other residents, is keen on sea fishing so there's a connection already. I wanted to ask you if it might be possible for you to arrive with a boat...'

'Yes, it might be. I fancy buying one anyway and one of the facets of active service is that you really don't spend any money, so I can afford it. Plus, of course, I'll get my army pension. I won't need much more than that to survive. I'll see what I can do!' Gary replied.

'Have you any family, Gary?' Sir David enquired.

'No, not really – the army has been my family. I'm on my own, and as you can imagine, I'm used to looking after myself.'

'OK then, Gary. Well, you arrive as soon as you can and we look forward to meeting you.'

'What are the other residents like, David?'

'Oh, you'll find friends; they are a very mixed bunch of interesting people. See you soon,' he said, putting the phone down. Sir David was pleased both to have secured another resident, albeit short term, and to have been of service.

***

Cat and Marie-Clare were making good progress in setting up a basic medical unit. A resident doctor would be ideal in the long term but they felt competent to offer an adequate service at this stage.

Jean-Paul was busy establishing an artwork shop. He wanted to run residential classes eventually. He was enjoying the space to explore the island and become familiar with its best views and perspectives at different times of day and in different light conditions. The couple were also working hard to ensure that they could cover for each other whenever necessary.

Megan was enjoying her new-found celebrity status and was pleased that her role in ensuring everyone's safety after the storm had been recognised. Together with her dad, they were improving and developing the farm on the island and would soon be ready to bring on some sheep. The chickens had settled well in the outbuilding and they had built their number up to forty. This supplied everyone on the island with eggs, as well as the pub and the café, and they still had some for Adra to sell in the shop. A small move along the road to independence had been achieved! Her grumpy brother was ready to take over the mainland farm and there was scope to help each other and to share equipment. Wyn still had some reservations about the scope for arable farming but had decided to start modestly by planting a few potatoes in the spring and experimenting with various crops. Beet, as animal feed for the sheep, was successful on his mainland farm so he hoped that it would prove viable on the island.

***

Gary had a rail warrant to travel to Conway to take a look at some boats. He had travelled with minimal belongings and equipment and hoped to secure a boat and use it to get himself to the island. He felt some form of rib would be appropriate, a bit like a modern military landing craft or the sort of boat used by the SBS. Not that he was planning any sort of assault from the sea!

The first boatyard he visited didn't seem very helpful so he moved on. Further along the coast, Gary found a larger yard, where the staff seemed more in tune with what he was looking for. He described his requirements and the salesman showed immediate interest; he knew of the island and was pleased to be able to help. The yard offered the full range of back up and service for every aspect of boat maintenance, like his personal REME attachment.

They agreed on a particular type of boat as the best fit for his requirements. They discussed terms and the salesman was prepared to take part payment and arrange credit to cover the remainder. So, together with a range of clothing and basic safety equipment and the minimum of induction, Gary drove out of the harbour and out to sea, heading for Anglesey.

The boat handled well and was reminiscent of craft he had used in the military. Gary gathered speed and enjoyed the freedom and exhilaration of the open sea. He soon covered the distance to the straits, where sailing against the tide did throw the boat around a little. Once he was clear of the coastline and out to sea, things became a little calmer.

Gary passed the first few islands on the way out to the

Island of Hawks and could make out the landing area as he approached. It looked like it needed some work. He did admit to himself that he was feeling quite apprehensive about this venture; it was way out of his comfort zone and not familiar territory. Despite Sir David's reassurance, Gary did wonder whether he would gel with the group.

He slowed the boat down and coasted in towards the shore. Gary quickly got out of the boat with his kit, momentarily wondering where his weapon and his mates were before smiling to himself and trying to stay relaxed. He had been through a lot on active service and the physical and emotional demands had eventually taken their toll. He had been lucky to avoid physical injury and was actually in very good shape, but mentally and psychologically he remained vulnerable. Not a state he was used to but one he had learnt to acknowledge and accept, although he still found it difficult to talk about it.

There was no reception committee, either friendly or hostile. Gary was able to secure the boat and pulled on his Bergen and carried the rest of his kit towards what looked little habitation. As he approached what appeared to be a pub, the prospect of a drink was appealing. He burst into the bar to introduce himself, much to everyone's surprise and delight.

He turned towards Adra, as the first person he saw. 'Hi, I'm Gary Watson. I believe you were expecting me?' he announced.

'Yes, sort of, but we weren't sure exactly when. Did you drive? Where have you left your car?' she asked.

'No, I came over by boat,' Gary replied.

'Oh, good for you. One of the local fishermen drop you off?'

'No, I came over in my own boat. It's secured in the harbour, such as it is.'

'Marvellous,' butted in Marie-Clare in her alluring French accent, 'so like a beach landing!'

'Yes, something like that.'

'Anyway, welcome,' said Rory, extending his hand.

'We understand that you're here for some R and R but could be useful to us too?'

'Yes, I hope so. Rest and Recuperation,' he responded, reading Marie-Clare's puzzled look.

Introductions were made and basics explained. Gary was shown his accommodation, which seemed to more than meet with his approval, and Adra offered to cook him some dinner later. He fancied one of her curries, which the others assured him were excellent. Rory offered to meet him in the bar for a drink later. It didn't take him long to unpack. That left him the afternoon to explore his surroundings. He set off in comfortable and familiar outdoor clothing to walk across to the edge of the island and to look out to sea.

Gary sat on a rock looking across the sea, trying to get his head round what was happening. He had been serving in Syria and had lost a good friend, which had hit him hard. Depression had set in and he needed a break. He had to acknowledge that actually the military had responded very well to his needs and that he had been well cared for. The notion of acceptance of trauma and psychological injury was more accepted now, he had found, and was less stigmatised.

Gary reflected on his time in hospital, then back in the UK in rehabilitation, and now arriving in this beautiful place with a bunch of misfits, dreamers and green freaks. He hoped that his initial impression would prove to be inaccurate and more to do with the harsh realities of the culture he had been used to than a true reflection of the group he now was living with.

Gary's senses were aroused and he turned suddenly to see a young woman approaching with a large dog. Hypersensitivity was a common problem for ex-soldiers and he had to learn not to interpret everything as a threat.

'Hi,' she called. 'You must be Gary, or do we call you Sgt?' Cat enquired as she laughed. 'I'm Cat,' she announced as she approached with her arms out stretched.

Gary wasn't used to such signs of immediate affection

but responded in kind.

'Can I join you?' asked Cat.

They sat on the rock together and just took in the view for a moment. It was cold but pleasant nevertheless.

'So, you are with us for a while, I understand, Gary?' asked Cat.

'Yes, that's right,' Gary replied.

'And after that?'

'Who knows?'

'OK, well... welcome for the moment!'

They sat for a while longer before the dog reminded them that actually this was meant to be a walk and they set off along the coast. Cat was looking after Bryn for the day whilst Megan was helping her dad fencing back on the farm on the mainland.

'So, do you think this is for you, Gary?' she enquired tentatively.

'I really don't know yet, Cat. But I'm grateful to be here.'

'No, need to be grateful.'

'Perhaps not, but people have been very kind and I love the house. Having moved around so much, a place to call my own is a novelty.'

'Well, take your time.'

'I intend to,' replied Gary.

'Did you leave anyone behind?' Cat asked.

'What? Family or women?'

'Yes, I suppose so.'

'No, neither. The army was my family and I've never had much luck with relationships. It doesn't help when you move around so much,' Gary explained.

Um, Cat wondered. *Well, you never know, girl*, she told herself.

They sat down again and watched the waves crashing.

'So, what happened to your real family?' Cat asked.

'I suppose I never actually had one, not in the conventional sense, anyway. My father got my mum pregnant then buggered off back to Jamaica and we never saw him again. She struggled and had a succession of abusive male partners. By the time I was sixteen, I'd had enough of it, so I lied about my age and applied to join the army. I knew nothing about being a soldier. I just wanted to get away. I'd seen the Guards Parade outside Buckingham Palace, so that's who I applied for; they were the first regiment that came into my head. It did me good, gave me some direction, a sense of discipline and some purpose in life. Without it, I suspect that I would have drifted into gangs and crime and ended up in prison. Life wasn't easy for a mixed-race lad growing up in a deprived council estate in the middle of London.'

***

Angus rang Sir David, hoping for an update on progress with the Hotel. His affairs in Skye were almost in order and he was keen to move to his new home on the Island of Hawks.

'Hi, Angus, it's good to hear from you. You're ringing for an update, I expect. Well, we are pretty much on track, as expected, to have the hotel ready for handover to you before Christmas. I expect you heard that we had a setback with some bad weather causing some damage, but you would be familiar with that, no doubt. The builders have been great and put in some extra hours to catch up. So, at this stage, it's ready when you are really. We can accommodate you in some form whenever you like and have you in the hotel shortly.'

'OK, David, that's great news. I'll finish off here and drive down to you early next week. I'm looking forward to it.'

'Good. We are looking forward to having you. Rory has signed contracts with two breweries – Titanic and Slater's from Staffordshire – to provide real ale and Mouse Head brewery to supply a local beer called Snowdonia. You might want to use some of your whiskey contacts, Angus,' added David.

***

Cat bumped into Gary again at the cafe. 'Hi, Gary, how are you?' she asked, trying not to sound too pleased to see him.

'Hi, Cat, I'm fine and you?' he replied eagerly.

'Coffee?' they both said together in unison and laughed.

'Then do you fancy another walk along the coast, Gary?'

'Yes, I do. I was thinking the same.'

After their coffee and a brief chat with Adra, they set off to explore a different section of the coast line.

'Ah, they do look good together,' declared Adra to Marie-Clare.

'Yes, I agree. Is there something in the air?'

'Who knows? I wasn't expecting *Love Island*!'

Gary and Cat walked along briskly in the fresh breeze and stopped to admire the view.

'How have your first few days been?' asked Cat, sympathetically.

'Oh, very good; people have been very welcoming. I enjoyed a curry with Adra on my first evening and a pint with Rory, who introduced me to his family.'

'Oh good, I'm pleased, and how are you feeling in yourself?' she asked.

'I think I'm OK. Thank you, nurse,' he replied, somewhat defensively.

They sat quietly for a while; Cat realising the importance of giving him time and space until she broke the silence anyway.

'Do you still see your mother, Gary?' asked Cat, wondering.

'No, she died years ago,' he replied.

'Oh, I'm sorry.'

'No need to be,' he responded. 'Hey, look out there: do you see that seal?' Gary cried, quickly changing the subject.

'Oh yes, seals on the island! I nearly joined the army you know, Gary, as a nurse. I didn't in the end – there was a boyfriend. He left me and joined up and wasn't the same when he came back from Afghanistan. He returned and was killed on his second tour. He never should have been sent back. The system let him down. I never wanted to join after that.'

'OK, how sad,' responded Gary, struggling to find the right words.

'How about you, have you been in love, Gary?'

'Love? I don't know. I don't think so.'

'So, what was it?'

'With women you mean? Oh, you know; women slip notes with their phone number into a Guardsman's pocket on duty. Some of the boys weren't keen, but if you were interested you were never short of a date – they'd pass the numbers on.'

'Didn't the girls object?'

'No, not really, one soldier in uniform looks much like another.'

'Gary!'

'I'm sorry Cat but that's how it was.'

'So you played the field?' Cat asked.

'Yes, I wasn't any good at what you might call relationships. I had no experience to draw on. I didn't know how to do the ordinary things like go shopping, cook dinner, or watch a film, for instance.'

'So, it was a physical thing?'

'Yes, I suppose so,' he replied, wondering how Cat might react.

'So, how would you treat me, Gary?' Cat asked directly.

'Oh, not like that!' he replied quickly.

'So, how's that then?'

'One, because you wouldn't let me and two, because you're worth more than that. All women should be treated well, I suppose.'

'Oh, is that a compliment?' she asked teasing him.

'Yes. Look, Cat, I'm getting too old to mess about – I need a bit of stability. I've seen enough suffering, tragedy and pain for one life time. I want to experience some joy. Some love, I suppose, but if I'm honest I'm not sure I know how to. So, if I took you out, I would have to learn to be a gentleman. Something I've never been!'

'Um, well you haven't asked me yet,' said Cat, holding his attention.

'OK. Miss Beeston, may I have the pleasure of accompanying you this evening?' Gary asked tentatively as she burst out laughing. Before he could feel deflated, she gave him his reply.

'Oh Gary, that's so formal. You're not asking me to the sergeants' mess ball!'

'Oh, I'm sorry. I did try to explain; I'm pretty new to this sort of thing, but Cat I really like you and want to spend some time with you,' he said sincerely.

Cat felt a rush of emotion as they stood closer and kissed for the first time.

Chapter Thirty-Two

Rory and Emma were enjoying their first impressions of island life. There was much to do, but that was exciting in itself. Poppy seemed to have taken to the move without undue concern. Having both parents around was a bonus. She was receiving plenty of attention. Whilst Emma missed Michaela and Pat from the village, she was getting on well with Betsy and her family since their recent arrival. Nevertheless, she looked forward to her friends joining them when they could.

Rory was able to make a start on his conservation project. He needed to catalogue sightings of all the island wildlife and fauna. He would need to get everyone on board, and also to record their observations. They were already aware of seals off the coast, a wide variety of bird life and some interesting rare plants. Rory wanted to set up some information boards for the tourists and visitors and a network of marked footpaths. He was also keen to develop the island's potential to host events for schools, conservation, naturalist and artist groups to come and stay on the island and indulge their hobbies and interests. There was also a need to undertake a programme of tree planting on a fairly large scale.

Bill and Gary got on famously. They shared a love of the sea and a wicked sense of humour. Bill's simple and light-hearted attitude to life and his positive disposition were both good for Gary. They soon planned a fishing trip together in Gary's new boat. Over breakfast at Adra's, the plan was hatched.

'What's for dinner tonight here, Adra?'

'Menu of the day, Gary.'

'What's that?' he enquired, not unreasonably.

'I haven't decided yet,' she replied, much to their amusement.

'OK, Adra, a suggestion: Welsh fish pie for all – a celebration night in for the team?'

'That's a good idea,' pitched in Bill as Ronan and Rory nodded from an adjacent table.

'Bill and I will catch the fish today, Welsh fish, that is, and we can start to bring you a regular supply, Adra. Build up some stock for the freezers.'

'Why? Are you planning for some kind of emergency, Gary?' asked Adra.

'It always pays to be prepared,' he replied, sounding very military.

'Um, no prizes for guessing your background!' she replied playfully.

'Adra, that wood burner over there... do you ever light it?' asked Gary.

'No, it was Rory's idea, but you may have noticed that there are virtually no trees on the island, so we have no logs.'

'What about driftwood? Or have you thought of burning dried sea weed?' Gary responded. 'Do we use the heat from the communal incinerator? That could take seaweed too?'

'Hear that Rory, Bear Grylls over there is getting us organised!'

'Not a bad idea though, Gary,' encouraged Rory. 'What could we utilise the heat for?'

'Look, both of you,' pointing to Rory and Ronan. 'Your kit is soaking. It's an island, and it's Wales, so we need a drying room, one for residents and one for guests at the hostel. There is a building already there near the incinerator that could use the energy. Fancy setting that up, guys? We'd need a hot water tank and some pipe work running around the edge of each drying bay furnished by the incinerator.'

Gary was already bringing his experience to bear.

Rory and Ronan were planning on writing some articles for distribution to the media, especially as it looked like it was going to be another wet and windy day, but Gary's ideas had started them thinking. A drying facility would be a real asset.

Rain or no rain, Gary and Bill set off suitably clad to tackle the seas while Adra planned her menu and Rory started sending the message around the houses – free residents supper in the pub tonight from seven o'clock. Ronan offered to play some Celtic folk music and Rory was determined to light the wood burner from available scraps of building timber. The plan was set in motion!

Emma and Betsy had planned to supervise all the children together in the communal hall, which was secure and dry, almost ready for handover. The two boys got on well with Poppy and were enjoying the freedom and informality of growing up in such a community, as were their parents in seeing the realisation of their dream unfolding. Communal childcare allowed maximum opportunity to address all the other needs of their new life, not least of which was to generate an income. Emma was conscious that she was not spending enough time promoting her business and was determined to redress the balance. Poppy was showing Bracken all around the new building and chattering away happily. Betsy was keen to spend more time writing too.

***

Out at sea, the boys were crashing through the waves heading for an area where they had been advised was good for fishing. Once they dropped anchor, the boat was reasonably steady as they set up their fishing rods and waited expectantly.

'How's it going, Gary?' asked Bill.

'Oh, OK, just hope the fish will bite,' he replied.

'No, I mean how's it going for you? How are you feeling and how are you settling in on the island?'

'Alright. I feel OK and I like the set up here! As I was told to expect, these are nice people, if a little naive to face a situation like this,' responded Gary.

'Good. Feeling OK is a start, Gary. I'm pleased for you. After what you've faced, it must be hard to adjust to civilian life…'

'Yes, I suppose so, Bill. It's hard to break old habits; not to constantly be on the alert, to want to site weapons in defence every time you stop, to constantly look to anticipate threats and to plan to take the fight to the enemy. Going fishing, setting up a drying room and walking along the coast isn't quite the same!' Gary acknowledged.

'No. Well, you take care,' Bill counselled, 'and there's that twinkle in your eye for a certain young lady…'

'Yes, I must admit I really like Cat. She's the sort of woman I need.'

'How do you mean?' queried Bill.

'Well, she seems to understand me. She's warm and sympathetic and can train me to be a civilised human being!' Gary suggested, thoughtfully.

'Well, good luck. Do you think you might stay, Gary?'

'I'm not sure, Bill. Not thinking too far ahead.'

Bill felt it was best not to push him, but to give Gary space to process his thoughts and decide on his future, although he hoped that Gary would stay – he brought something unique to the group. Then his thoughts were interrupted as he noticed a strong pull on one of the fishing rods.

By the time they returned to the island, Bill and Gary had caught enough fish to feed them all for a while! They had worked well together and had enjoyed the experience. A young woman waited anxiously for their return, concerned for their safety in such rough weather. Bill could sense her unease as they landed and secured the boat but the moment was lost on Gary; he was focused on landing his catch and getting the boat properly tied down.

As they bought the fish into the kitchen, much to everyone's admiration, Bill gently prompted Gary to go over and reassure Cat that they were alright. He looked a little puzzled but took Bill's advice and went to speak to Cat first before thinking about sorting out his kit and getting changed.

We really need that drying room, he thought.

***

A car drew up at the pub and in walked Angus after travelling from Skye.

'Hello everyone, I'm Angus Cameron. I look forward to meeting you all.'

'Hi,' said Adra, as the first to greet him. 'Come on in. We knew you were coming along soon. You've timed it well – you can settle into your room at the hostel first and then we are all meeting this evening here for a bit of a knees-up.'

'Great, I love a good ceilidh!' he replied.

'Ronan is even going to play some Celtic music!'

'Very cultural. OK, I'll unload my stuff,' Angus replied.

'I'll give you a hand,' offered Gary, still soaking wet.

'Dressed for the weather, I see,' said Angus, laughing as the two men got stuck into unloading Angus's kit, before Gary went off for a shower.

Cat smiled, thinking to herself, *he's such a typical bloke, but I'll have to train him.* Her dad had been in the army, he was in the Royal Engineers, not the shooting end of the army, but he had dealt with many explosions and witnessed first-hand the devastating impact modern weapons can have on the human body. He found it difficult to talk about his experiences too. Cat had to acknowledge that she felt an attraction to Gary, but she was taking her time. She had been hurt before and was a little cautious now, although she was relieved that Gary seemed to need to take things slowly too. *Is he the one?* she pondered. She thought he might be!

Angus took a walk around the hotel. It was impressive. A mixture of renovation and new build, tastefully done to accommodate a modest twelve guests for bed and breakfast, or with dinner included. He was excited about the prospect of making his mark on his own hotel. Well, as the manager at least, if not the owner.

After twenty years in the business, he felt ready to take

the helm. He would have to think of a name, appoint some staff and set the tone for the establishment. Relaxed, welcoming and cosmopolitan was his ambition, plus of course serving great food, wines and ales. Appointing a decent chef would be a priority, but there was time for all of that yet. He wanted to gain a feel for the place before naming it, and have some say in the final details of the building.

Angus came from an island background, having been born and brought up on Mull, and knew the joys and demands of island life. His parents had been in the hotel industry. He had travelled extensively as a young man and worked for ten years in New Zealand before moving back to Scotland to take up a post on the Isle of Skye. He knew that he would miss Scotland but that this was a new chapter in his life. He looked forward to the evening entertainment and an introduction to his fellow islanders as he poured himself a nice pint of Titanic Iceberg.

Michaela and Pat were pleased to inform Emma that they had sold their house and would be in a position to move to the island shortly. Emma had really missed them and looked forward to being reunited. There was also one more piece of news – Michaela was pregnant and expecting their first child!

Chapter Thirty-Three

The party was a great success. Everyone enjoyed the opportunity to learn more about their fellow islanders. Rory was pleased that their efforts in selection seemed to have paid off with a good mix of people, skills, interests and aspirations, but most of all they were people who could work together.

The drinks flowed as Adra served her fish pie made from fresh local ingredients. The children played before falling asleep and Ronan actually was quite good on his various instruments to give the occasion a Celtic theme.

Gary stood looking across the room at Cat. He felt compelled to be near her, thought about her constantly and was not sure what was going on, or if he could handle it. She noticed his attention and walked across to him.

'You can talk to me, you know, instead of staring like a love-struck teenager!' said Cat, looking directly into his eyes.

'Yes, I'm sorry, Cat. I have never felt this way before. I'm not sure I understand it, but I know it feels good.'

Give him time, she thought, wisely. *Don't rush it.*

Adra had noticed the exchange of glances and was confident that she knew what it meant.

Marie-Clare and Jean-Paul were dancing and Megan didn't know quite what to make of it all. *Maybe some more young men might arrive in time*, she hoped.

Rory drew Emma close as they looked around the room. They felt so happy and contented; this was more than they could have hoped for. This was a community. This felt like what life should be about.

***

The following day, everyone agreed that the party had been a great success and that regular 'dining in nights' ought to become a standing feature. Adra had done very well but it was obvious that trying to run the pub operation on her own, albeit having everyone chipping in, was unsustainable. They needed some staff.

Rory had recruited Gary's help to start charting out some footpaths and to think about signposting and mapping. Gary had soon established a good sense of the island's geography and had walked its full length, including climbing the modest hill in the centre. 'Footpaths,' he said, 'usually followed a natural course through a landscape.' He anticipated finding existing tracks rather than creating new ones. He was right, of course, and the beginning of a plan for a waymarked route emerged.

'Look, see that!' exclaimed Gary as a rabbit shot across their path. 'Another natural source of food!'

'Really?' responded Rory, not being familiar with that particular delicacy.

'Yes, if rabbits are established here, Rory, then we can harvest them. I love rabbit stew and, if nothing else, they can provide meat for the dogs.' Right on cue, Bracken saw another rabbit and set chase, quickly running it down.

Bracken efficiently dispatched his prey and proudly wagged his tail to indicate his quarry.

'How do you cook it, Gary?' Rory asked.

'On an open fire, usually!' he responded smiling, 'but you have to gut and skin it first.'

Rory looked forward to his forthcoming introduction to survival skills as they walked back towards the pub with rabbit in hand. On the kitchen table, Gary demonstrated how to prepare the animal for the pot as Adra peeled some vegetables to cook with it.

'Rabbit stew is an option on the menu tonight!' she announced.

'Mr Survival here reckons we can live like kings on what we can forage from the land and sea,' declared Rory as Adra laughed and the name stuck.

'Mr Survival, indeed!'

***

Sir David had suggested a further meeting to review progress and to establish some priorities, with an outline schedule for future work. Rory convened the available members of the group as Sir David attempted to summarise the current state of affairs.

'I'm very pleased to say, as we approach Christmas, that we are now ahead of target with most of the initial phase of the building programme complete. We have full use of the pub/cafe/shop, the communal hall and sufficient housing for our current needs. The hostel is ready for use and is due to be finally completed to offer accommodation for up to twenty people by early in the New Year. The hotel is also near completion, albeit a little late, and we now have the services of Angus to start to accommodate some guests. Some early bookings are already in place and we envisage a formal opening before the spring. It will need a name, if you would like to give that some thought.'

'That's really good!' responded Emma as others agreed.

'Megan, would you like to update us on developments at the farm?'

'Yes, of course. It's going very well, actually, after the initial set back with the loss of the chickens. My dad and I have moved into the farmhouse and most of the outbuildings, including workshop space, are now viable. The barn is due to be erected when the weather calms down in spring or summer. We now have forty laying hens and a cockerel so, in time, we will be able to raise our own chicks. Fifty sheep are due to arrive next week and Dad feels confident that they can roam freely on the island without undue risk to them. If we use the services of our own ram from the mainland farm, we could be producing lambs to use or sell later next year,' announced Megan, and her comments were greeted with a round of applause.

'As regards arable production, Dad is more sceptical about our prospects, but he aims to start modestly planting a potato crop in March and experimenting with other crops throughout the year. This opens up the prospect of servicing the pub café shop and the hotel in due course, as well as producing some feed for the sheep,' Megan concluded.

'Marvellous. Thank you, Megan,' replied Sir David. The group acknowledged the arrival of Gary and his boat, which had enhanced the prospects for fishing. They also discussed the progress made with both supplying and selling their own green energy, together with Gary's suggestion about harvesting the heat from the incinerator.

'So, suggestions for tasks for the coming period up to the spring?' invited David.

After minimal debate, the following priorities were established:

1. Complete the fitting out of the hotel.
2. Expand the use of the pub/cafe/shop.
3. Erect the farm's barn.
4. Look to develop income generation through the above, fishing and party bookings for courses and tourism.
5. Set up the drying rooms.
6. Work on Rory's conservation project, including tree planting.
7. Complete a health and safety review, and establish an evacuation plan.
8. Start to consider longer term management arrangements.

'What about expanding our number and building more housing?' enquired Bill.

'Good point,' Sir David replied. 'Actually, I have some news on that front. I have been in discussion with the Home Office, who are looking for opportunities to place Syrian refugees. If we were to accept say ten people, there would be the possibility of quite generous financial inducements. That could be a welcome boost to our funds but wouldn't come without risk. We would have little control over precisely who came, or indeed what condition they might be in, or how well they might adapt to this environment. Initially, at least, they could be accommodated in the hostel, so we already have the capacity.'

The room fell silent for a moment before Marie-Clare was the first to offer an opinion. 'As a foreign national myself, I welcome the prospect of a more international dimension, and I do have sympathy for these poor people who nobody seems to want.'

There were some nods and some looks of reservation.

'Likewise, I sympathise with these people, but I think we have to be realistic about what we might be taking on. After what they've been through, many of them will be in an awful state, physically, mentally and emotionally. True, we could do them a real service, but I don't think that we should expect them to offer us much in return, at least not initially,' offered Gary.

'Yes, I agree and ten seems a lot to me. It could destabilise the group after we've made such a good start. Aren't there any remaining recruits still selected and due to join us, David?' asked Bill to nods of approval.

'Actually, no, not really. Hayley and Marcus, Emma and Rory's friends from their village who ran the pub, are still due to join us, but then that's it. The other candidates have effectively fallen by the wayside, for various reasons. We do hope to attract people as short stays on temporary work contracts, but that is no substitute. Wyn told me last night that a young couple from the local farming community on the mainland have approached him and shown an interest. They have three children, two girls and a boy, aged four, three and six months. So, unless we start the whole recruitment exercise again, the Syrian people are a timely option,' explained Sir David.

'A diverse community was part of the original vision,' Rory reminded them. 'I don't think we should shy away from it but embrace it. We are not looking to escape from the world but to enhance it.'

'I would have to say, from my experience on Skye, that foreign workers were great. Generally, we struggled to recruit sufficient local labour, which might not apply here, and particularly the Eastern Europeans were a real asset. Most of them spoke reasonable English and worked incredibly hard. I have no direct experience of Syrians, but I wouldn't dismiss the idea,' added Angus.

After further discussion, it was tentatively agreed to allow David to explore the idea further and negotiate on their behalf, looking to recruit initially five Syrian refugees to complement the twenty-eight people already committed, making a community of thirty-three in all. That seemed sensible – allowing time to generate some income before committing to building further housing, albeit that it would be short of the target set for occupation by autumn the following year. However, getting it right, they all agreed, was more important than rigidly adhering to the timetable.

Chapter Thirty-Four

Next to arrive were Michaela and Pat, together with Hayley and Marcus, Emma and Rory's friends from their time in Coppermere. Michaela and Pat brought a range of craft experience to add to the pool of skills in the community. Michaela was a competent wood turner and dress maker. Pat was a painter and an accomplished chef. Angus was hopeful that he might be the answer to his plans to start his hotel staff recruitment in the kitchen. He needed a good chef and might just have acquired one!

Hayley and Marcus would provide a welcome boost to the pub in working alongside Adra. Their mechanical expertise could also be useful in providing an in-house maintenance and repair facility in one of the workshops at the farm.

The new couples were pleased with their allotted accommodation and very happy to join the community, at last after some delay in completing their arrangements back in Coppermere, including selling their property.

Over the following few days, the first group of temporary workers from Europe arrived. Both a Polish and a Romanian man had agricultural experience and came to help on the farm. Two Spanish female students and one male aimed to improve their English and were prepared to work in the hotel or the pub/café, waiting or cleaning. They were all accommodated in the hostel and were due to stay for three months.

Sir David was pleased to conclude his negotiations with the Home Office regarding the Syrian refugees. He was fortunate to secure the services of an experienced doctor, who wanted to live on the island and had been offered work as a GP on the mainland for four days per week, allowing him to run a clinic on the island for a further day. This could complement Cat's role as the island's nurse. In addition, four young men were due to join the community who were described as able-bodied, wanting to settle in the

UK and keen to work. Doing exactly what Sir David anticipated could be worked out later, once they had some opportunity to acclimatise themselves with their new surroundings.

This would take the total island resident population to approaching forty, Sir David considered.

Enquires about the potential future of the church on the island also took a step forward with the agreement of those consulted in principle to open a multi-faith centre. Firm bids would need to be established from as many religious groups as possible to create a viable plan and to bring it to fruition. A delegation from Liverpool University had also asked to visit to explore the details of their research proposals.

Rory and Emma were conscious of the number of aspects of the project all moving forward at the same time and were keen to keep themselves grounded. Inducting the new members would be important in order to keep the sense of identity within the community that had already been established.

The following few weeks had its challenges in settling in the new members. Sadly, as Gary had predicted, the four Syrian men were seriously traumatised by their experiences. They spoke little English and arrived simply with the few ragged clothes they stood up in. They had been forced off their land, set about an horrendous journey across North Africa, been taken advantage of by people traffickers, and had attempted to cross the Mediterranean three times before being reluctantly accepted in Italy. Three months followed in a squalid camp with no contact with their family back home, or even confirmation of who had survived the onslaught from government troops, before being identified for passage to England. They had been processed at an immigration centre in Kent and allocated to the island project as a suitable placement for resettlement.

The whole community united behind admirable attempts to reassure and assist then. Clothing and personal effects were found and good food and medical assessment provided. Marie-Clare instigated a programme of teaching basic English and, together with Cat, offered counselling through the services of an interpreter.

It transpired that one of the four was not from Syria at all but had travelled from Iraq, and he was not related to the other three, who had effectively adopted him and told the authorities that the four men were all cousins. It soon became clear that it would take some time to stabilise these men and that patience and understanding would be required with little or no expectation of reciprocation.

Although this was broadly what the group had expected, it was nevertheless shocking to be confronted with its reality. The doctor had fared much better, using wealth and contacts to escape from his country in the early stages of the conflict and finding assistance in Turkey initially before arriving in the UK.

The two workers from Poland and Romania, by contrast, spoke quite good English and soon adapted to farming practices on the island. They worked hard, were grateful for the opportunity, and the chance to be able to send money back home to support their families. The young Spanish students were enthusiastic and soon engaged with the project, taking opportunities to help Rory with his conservation work and Bill and Gary on their fishing trips, as well as working in the hotel. They were a joy to have on board.

Rory was making progress with his network of footpaths and had started to catalogue sightings of wildlife, including seals and otters, together with a wide variety of bird life.

Gary and Bill made a start on setting up the drying rooms, which given the weather, was an obvious priority. The pipe work wasn't complicated and the building with two separate bays was already identified and ready for use, so it wasn't long before it became operational! It was soon in use and became a welcome addition to their limited facilities.

***

Cat had taken on some hours as a nurse in the GP practice where the Syrian doctor was working. With that and her commitments back at the island, there hadn't been much time left to spend with Gary. In a way, that had suited them both, allowing their relationship to grow slowly.

Gary was still struggling to recognise and manage his emotions and Cat was trying hard both to understand and to help him. Taking the opportunity to walk along the coast, they were able to discuss their feelings.

'How are you finding island life now, Gary?' Cat asked, whilst holding on firmly to his arm in the strong wind.

'Oh, I'm enjoying it, Cat. I've decided to take up the offer of staying the full six months. I think it's doing me good.'

'Do you miss the army?' she asked.

'Of course, to some extent. It had been my saviour and my life, but I still feel that it was the right decision to leave. I need to move on and find a new life. After all, I've found you!' he said awkwardly, not used to expressing such emotions.

'Ah, and I've found you too, Gary Watson.' Cat replied, squeezing his arm hard.

'As I've shared with you, Cat, I'm not used to having such strong feelings of attachment to women. Of course, relationships in the army between blokes were close. You form a bond with people when your lives depend on each other, but that is different. It hit me hard when my best mate was killed right next to me,' he paused and struggled not to get emotional.

'Let the feelings go, Gary. It's OK,' Cat tried to encourage him.

'You see I don't remember ever really being loved or giving love,' Gary announced, surprising himself with his sudden insight.

'You didn't finish telling me about your mother, Gary.

You mentioned she died young, but what happened? Didn't she love you as a child?'

Gary took in a deep breath; dare he tell her?

After collecting his thoughts, Gary replied tentatively, 'I suppose she did in her own way, but it didn't feel much like love to me. She was always so stressed just keeping going.' Then he paused again.

'She was killed, Cat. Murdered by one of her abusive partners,' Gary disclosed quietly. 'I was serving in Afghanistan at the time. If I'd been in the UK, I'm sure I would have killed the bastard, so it was a good job I wasn't.'

'Oh Gary, that's awful. How do you deal with that?' she exclaimed rhetorically through tears as they approached the farm on the far side of the island.

'Like most of my emotions, Cat, it's boxed off and buried in the back of my mind,' Gary replied honestly.

'Then maybe it's time to think about unpacking them?' Cat suggested, carefully.

Chapter Thirty-Five

December 2018

Christmas arrived! The whole group made a real effort to integrate everyone's different family and cultural Christmas traditions and to include those who didn't usually celebrate the occasion. Turkey remained on the menu, but many other ideas from around the world were also incorporated into a celebration of community, joy and fellowship. Wyn provided a tree from his old farm; Adra baked all sorts of goodies; Bill and Gary made a special effort to catch different fish, including a small shark; and all the children played all day, enjoying each other's company.

Everyone pitched in with the chores and it didn't seem any trouble at all. Some of the group elected to return to their home area and families, but most stayed to celebrate their first Christmas together on the island.

Emma was already feeling the pressure of carrying the new baby and there was still six months to go! She looked forward to its arrival but understandably felt some anxiety about the impending birth, although her first experience of pregnancy and birth had got well. She was not due until June, but for now, there was a need to just keep going. Bracken would patiently sit with her when she was feeling tired, as if he understood. He could be such a comfort at times.

On Boxing Day, most of the group set out for a walk together with all the dogs. Megan rode the quad bike and trailer to transport the children when they'd had enough, which of course, as soon as they saw the possibility of trailer rides, wasn't very long at all!

They returned to enjoy a table full of different foods, from the shark steaks to curry, pizza and tapas. Wyn and Megan thought it was a bit strange, but most of the group loved it. Gary and Cat sat quietly for a moment, holding hands on one of the sofas while Adra gave them admiring looks. Emma and Rory kissed under the mistletoe and Megan showed more than a passing interest in one of the Syrian lads. The two Spanish girls seemed quite happy together and Marie-Clare and Jean-Paul seemed to dance all day.

Gifts had been exchanged, best wishes offered and a sense of optimism about the future shared. The project was beginning to feel like it was a success. In a relatively short space of time, they had set up and created a community in the spirit that they originally envisaged. Emma and Rory were proud of their achievement. There had been challenges, setbacks and disappointments, but they were pleased that they had been able to overcome them.

After the festivities, a party of largely older men from the Midlands, old friends since university days, stayed at the hostel and walked Rory's paths and enjoyed fishing and quad bike riding. They ate breakfast in the cafe and dinner in the pub, which all helped to generate business. They walked to the top of the hill in the centre of the island to enjoy the spectacular views across to Snowdon and the Carneddau range and they enjoyed taking photographs and sharing their experiences with the islanders in the bar afterwards.

Other groups followed. Working groups, business groups, friendship groups and different sports clubs all started to make bookings. Wyn was able to press on with developments on the farm and introduce five pigs and some goats to the mix of livestock. Hayley and Marcus had established a basic workshop at the farm and were busy rebuilding an old quad bike to add to the fleet of vehicles available for communal use.

Gary completed his work on an emergency evacuation plan and, as part of his safety review, pointed out to the group that, so far, they had made no serious provision for the eventuality of fire. He invited the local fire commander to visit the island, who confirmed that it would be unlikely that a fire engine would be able to get across to the island,

and as it certainly could not be guaranteed, they would need to make their own basic provision.

Taking advice, Gary and Bill set about constructing a series of fire points with water buckets, sand and a simple alarm system, using football rattles. Access to water obviously wasn't a problem on an island and a limited number of hosepipes were strategically placed to be able to access water and direct it to the various buildings, if required. The fire commander inspected their work and regarded their arrangements as satisfactory as a first response. Angus had experience of similar plans working on many of the Scottish islands and agreed that their efforts were likely to be sufficient, at least initially.

Wyn was pleased to confirm that the young farming couple, Cerwyn and Hafren from the mainland, who had registered an interest, were keen to go ahead and move onto the island, initially in the hostel with a view to building a second farmhouse in time. They wanted to take a lead in developing the arable side of the farm. When they arrived and mentioned their cousin, Craig, who was looking for premises to expand his micro-brewery, the community were eager to recruit him as well, so soon Island Ales was born and in full production! They could supply all the island required and sell their produce widely on the mainland.

Sir David and their accountant had worked out a formula for a sort of community charge, levied by agreement on all business earnings on the island, to fund community requirements. He was pleased to be able to announce that, with sponsorship, venture capital, government grants, conservation and environmental contributions and their own resources, that the financial side of the project was established on a firm footing.

***

Different members of the group elected to help Bill and Gary with their fishing exploits, with some taking to it better than others. Cat decided that it was time she took a turn and supported Gary in his endeavours. He was, of course, pleased to be able to encourage her interest. They set off from the landing station that the boys had built on a relatively calm but cold day. Gary was keen to ensure that all necessary precautions and safety equipment was available to anyone who joined them on his boat. Cat felt a little apprehensive, not being a practised sailor, but was prepared to sample the experience.

Gary competently steered the boat out to sea on their usual route to their familiar fishing grounds. When anchor dropped, Cat did admit to feeling somewhat queasy as the boat rolled, tossed and turned in the lively sea. The boys helped her set up a fishing rod and, between them, they managed to catch a good supply of fish – enough to keep the islanders and their business interests supplied.

Cat enjoyed just spending some time with Gary, and Bill was very considerate in giving them the space they needed. Although it was cold, wet and windy, the three of them persevered against the adverse conditions.

Although she didn't complain, by early afternoon Gary could see that Cat had had enough and decided that it was time to turn back to shore. Bill agreed and they secured their catch and set off back towards the island, with Gary steering the boat. Bill went to the back of the boat to discreetly have a wee and to make a call back to the island to confirm that they were heading for home as the weather started to deteriorate further. When he turned back to face the front of the boat, he assumed that Cat had gone to sit with Gary in the cockpit. After a short while, he decided to join them.

'Hi, Bill, everything OK?' Gary asked as he appeared behind him.

'Yes, fine,' he replied.

'Where's Cat?' asked Gary.

'I assumed that she was with you,' he replied as a look of horror flashed across Gary's face, and it was at that moment that Gary Watson, sergeant, ex-Grenadier Guard realised what love meant. He felt an overwhelming rush of emotion and motivation. He was in no doubt that having found Cat there was no way he could be without her now.

'Where is she, Bill? Where is she, for God's sake!' he cried.

Both men desperately looked around the small craft, soon reaching the obvious conclusion. While Bill had been distracted, she must have fallen overboard.

Light was fading, the weather deteriorating and suddenly matters became very serious.

'No one will survive long in these conditions, Bill. If she's gone overboard, we have to find her!' Gary shouted as he quickly turned the boat around and started to head back towards the fishing grounds.

At least they knew that Cat was properly dressed in suitable clothing for a wet fishing trip and that her life jacket would keep her upright. Gary had confirmed with her that she could swim and had explained basic safety procedures in the event of various situations arising – 'man overboard' being one of them.

The immediate action expected of a swimmer in this situation was to activate the light on their life jacket to make it easier for any rescue attempt to identify them in the sea. As Gary raced back as quickly as he could, both men looked out desperately for any sign of it.

Gary instructed Bill to take the helm as he got ready to drive in to rescue her as soon as they could find her. He stayed calm, drawing on all his experience of difficult, dangerous and demanding situations, but this one was different. This one mattered far more. He knew that he simply couldn't lose her – he had to rescue her!

'There, there!' cried Bill. 'A light bobbing up and down in the water.'

In an instant, Gary had dived into the open sea and swam quickly and efficiently towards her while Bill steadied the boat in readiness for the return of his two companions.

By this time, Cat was losing consciousness in the cold

water. She knew Gary would do all he could to get to her as she waited, desperately hoping to see the return of the boat. Then she saw it with all its lights blazing out, and yes, she saw a body swimming towards her.

Safely, securely and with practised relative ease, Gary took control. As he approached Cat, he shouted to her to stay calm and that he would swim them both back to the boat. She could hardly hear him but assumed that he would reach her shortly. He held out his strong arms and secured her tightly in his grip, holding her as high as he could and as far out of the water as possible while he turned efficiently and set off at best speed back to safety. Bill was anxiously watching events from the boat and steered her as close as he could to be able to receive the two of them back on board.

Feeling safe in Gary's arms, Cat relaxed and, by the time he brought her to the side of the boat, she was unconscious. Quickly in the half-light, the two men pulled her aboard and Gary climbed into the boat, ordering Bill to steer back to the island as fast as possible, while he ensured that Cat was still alive. The over-powering feelings of love that were shooting through his body were unfamiliar to Gary but he knew that he had to save her – that she could survive.

He moved closer to start mouth to mouth resuscitation when she spluttered and opened her eyes. She was alive! Gary kissed her then rang to shore to have the doctor on standby as he did his best to keep her warm. He had no way of knowing how well she might have coped with her ordeal or how much sea water she might have swallowed, but he knew that she was alive and that now she would be safe.

Chapter Thirty-Six

Gary was well aware that the cold can kill and that, in the circumstances, Cat was in danger of slipping into hyperthermia. The rescuer's dilemma, however, is whether to strip the casualty out of their wet clothes and into dry ones, to best keep them warm, although it would risk exposure in the process. Or whether to insulate them as best they could over their wet clothes to avoid that problem but accept that, being wet, their efforts would be compromised.

In any event, for Gary, the choice was made for him as they had no spare dry clothes, but he did have several heat pads that, once opened, radiated moderate heat immediately. Quickly Gary applied one to Cat's chest, over her heart, and one to her back. Then he wrapped her in an insulation blanket and held her close, sheltering her from the wind.

As she slipped in and out of consciousness, he encouraged her to take a warm drink whenever she could to keep her going until Bill could land the boat. Fortunately, the doctor was waiting as Bill brought the boat ashore and, as Gary expected, drove her straight to the medical centre. Once there, with Marie-Clare's help, they placed her in a warm bath to raise her core temperature, albeit slowly.

Gary felt much better after a hot shower and immediate returned to Cat's aid. The doctor had checked her over and concluded that Gary's efforts to keep her temperature from falling below a critical level had been successful. He felt that her chances of a full recovery were good. What she needed now was some rest and to stay warm. Evidently, they had been lucky!

Adra took charge and gave Gary his instructions.

'Now, young man, you are to stay with this young lady and guard her all night, watch over her and keep her warm.' Seeing the look in his eye, Adra added, 'You'll have to wait, Gary, but you must hold her close and keep her warm.'

Gary looked back at her knowingly, saluted smartly and turned to the right.

'Now, Mr Survival, you do your duty!' Adra ordered and knew that he would comply.

Sleep proved to be fitful. By the morning, the evident exchange of warm glances between Gary and Cat left Adra in little doubt that more than just sleep had been enjoyed between them and she felt pleased for them both that they'd found each other. They made a lovely couple, she thought.

Later in the day, once Cat was sufficiently rested, Gary was able to ask her if she could remember what had happened out at sea.

'I saw Bill go to the rear of the boat, I guessed what for. I needed to go myself but it's not so easy for us girls. I then learned over the side to feel how cold the water was, my feet slipped and the next thing I knew was that I was out of the boat and floating freely in the sea. I remembered what you had told me about the light on my jacket, so I activated that as instructed. Then I suppose I just waited to find out,' Cat explained.

'Find out what?' he asked.

'How much you loved me!' Cat replied. 'And now I know.'

'And so do I,' Gary replied.

Chapter Thirty-Seven

January 2019 proved to be cold on the island and another reminder of just what they had taken on. The group continued to gel as a team and steady progress was made over the remainder of the winter, with business picking up in the hotel, the pub, the café and the shop, as more tourists came to explore this new experimental community.

It was not for everyone, however, and after trying to persevere, Michaela and her partner had to admit that they were struggling, and were thinking of leaving the island to return to a more conventional life on the mainland. Michaela wasn't experiencing the easiest of pregnancies and was concerned about the prospect of giving birth on the island. Their doctor, Farid Ghani, tried his best to reassure her, but she remained concerned that neither he nor Cat could guarantee they would be available on the island when the time came. She would also be some distance away from her family.

Emma was particularly sad and disappointed to hear of the prospect of them leaving but could understand their reservations. Angus also had to admit that he didn't want to lose his chef. Pat had settled into the role well. Adra had helped him, with both of them learning from each other. Angus thought he had better allocate more of Adra's time to be spent at the hotel rather than the pub, where Hayley and Marcus could cope, just in case Michaela and Pat did decide to leave and he lost his chef.

Emma, Rory and Poppy continued to grow closer and enjoy the precious time together that their new lifestyle afforded them. Emma could start to feel the baby moving about inside her, as if impatient to meet the world. Despite all that had happened, Emma still felt some sense of regret that her mum had not lived long enough to be with them at this critical time. She felt confident that, one way or another, Rory would get her to hospital in time for the birth, if that was necessary, although she really wanted to have this child on the island.

Poppy was growing up fast and would be two in June so they would need to start thinking about having a plan in place for her schooling when the time came. They had to accept that the community was too small as yet to justify establishing a school on the island, but they had talked about home tuition with Marie-Clare and Cat, which was a realistic alternative.

Emma was keen to avoid any need to travel back and forth to the mainland on a daily basis, if at all possible. Everyone was far more safety-conscious after what had happened to Cat. Farid, their doctor, had strongly advised Gary not to run any more fishing trips with novices in the winter, restricting that opportunity to the better weather.

Once Cat was fully recovered from her ordeal, she and Gary decided to move in together, which would release a house for Cerwyn, Hafren and their three children. It would be a bit of a squeeze for them, but it would be better than being in the hostel. It suited the single workers alright but was not so good for families.

Cat and Gary were pleased to announce to the group that they were now officially together, which was greeted with joy as the group all offered their congratulations! Cat was also estranged from her family and felt a degree of regret that they would not share in her news. Her parents had separated and divorced when she was young. Cat stayed with her mother initially but, after she had left home at eighteen, her mother had eventually settled in Canada. Her father had remarried and she hadn't heard from either of them for years. Like Gary, Cat had to learn to be independent and self-sufficient from an early age, and that was another reason why her new-found experience with Gary was so special to her. She found the prospect of having someone to share her life with really exciting.

***

As winter subsided and spring started to emerge, it was a welcome relief for all the islanders from the harsh realities of the exposure to bad weather inherent in their new life style. Most of them had not envisaged the degree of the challenge involved. Angus and Wyn, with his daughter Megan, were unsurprisingly the best prepared to withstand the conditions, with most of the others having to learn and adapt rapidly.

For the refugees, of course, it was even more of a contrast with the climate and weather conditions that they had been used to. Farid had adapted reasonably well but the other three men had found it much harder. However, they were making progress with Marie-Clare, in learning to speak and read in English, and had started to do some work helping in the hotel.

Their sense of relief at having been accepted and having found a home was apparent to all. Not all the islanders, however, found it so easy to understand the refugee's sadness at being forced out of their own country. Being so far away from family and friends and not knowing who, if anyone, of their loved ones was still alive was so hard to bear.

***

The time came for the temporary workers from overseas to return home and for new people to arrive. The Spanish girls had enjoyed their stay, had fitted in well and had become accepted as a couple. The young man had not embraced the experience as readily and was eager to return home. The Eastern Europeans were happy to extend their stay and had made a useful contribution to the farm. Their earnings were much higher in the UK than at home, which allowed them to send generous support back to their families, helping to ease the pain of separation.

Emma and Rory prepared to welcome three young French women who, it was hoped, would make the most of the opportunity and adapt quickly. With spring in the air, they would enjoy a different experience of the island over the coming months. Their arrival would take the resident population up to thirty-five, including eight children. *Maybe the idea of a school in the long term isn't so unreasonable*, thought Emma. She decided to talk to Marie-Clare again and suggest that they open negotiations with the local council to explore the options thoroughly. Free schools, of course, were also an option, she thought, but the idea of home tuition appealed to her. Those children already of school age were being provided for on the mainland but the realities of daily travel were not ideal.

On the same day Rory received an unexpected enquiry about potential residence on the island. Rory hadn't heard anymore from Rhys after their last contact, about any progress with his research. It appeared that the idea had faltered due to problems securing suitable support and funding. Rhys had emailed him however, to tell him that he'd been successful in an application for a transfer to work at Bangor University and that they had agreed to fund the research in full. He would be due to start in September, at the beginning of the academic year. As such he would need somewhere to live locally and wondered how Rory might feel about him asking to become a resident on the island? He mentioned the prospect to Emma later and she agreed that would be an interesting development and to put it to the community at the next suitable opportunity. Emma wondered whether Rhys's presence on the island might be an unwelcome distraction for Rory in reminding him of his past working life, but Rory assured her that rather than resent Rhys's presence he felt that he would welcome it. Actually, it felt like a very fitting end to a career in the probation service. He quite looked forward to the prospect of some interesting debates with Rhys about criminal justice, social policy and their respective experiences, but that would be for the future. It would be for the group to decide, but he felt confident that they would approve the application.

Chapter Thirty-Eight

Rory and Emma sat outside their house on the island on a pleasant evening in early spring. Poppy was playing happily around them with Bracken. They reflected on their progress and their achievements and how all the effort had been worth it.

They had managed to establish an independent community approaching forty people from different parts of the world, from various backgrounds, with different complementary skills, who could work together. The business aspect of the project had been a success, with a healthy number of bookings, both for the hotel and the hostel, early encouraging signs of developing a number of craft initiatives, and the pub acting as the hub of the community. The farm was still expanding, with the aspiration to move towards self-sufficiency on the island in time.

They had plans to build further housing and attract more residents, and had already secured outline planning permission and the offer of further funding. They had learnt some harsh lessons about the need for mutual support and had benefited from the healthy outdoor life style. They both felt less stressed and more contented. They had learnt to live with less and value what they had more. Their two part-time incomes had proved to be sufficient as their real needs were modest.

In the longer term, the island would need to establish more permanent governance arrangements and allow the management group to stand down. With residents making an initial contribution to join the project, giving a percentage of any earnings, and purchasing their own individual houses on the island, the model had good prospects of remaining sustainable. Sir David had done an excellent job in helping to steer the project in the right direction and on a sound footing, but he too was ready to move on.

The conservation project had more than met its initial targets and had secured funding for Rory's post for a further eighteen months. Emma's business realistically had lost some momentum, but she was confident that would be retrievable. They had a fledgling medical service, the outline idea of establishing home tuition for the children's education and the prospect of reopening the church as a multi-faith centre.

Gary had added his considerable experience to the project and it had helped him refocus his life. Emma and Rory were delighted to hear that he had decided to extend his stay again, beyond the initial three and then six months, to a more permanent arrangement. He had been discharged from the army on good terms and had secured his full pension. His plans to run fishing trips and open a scuba diving school were still only embryonic, but he was confident they were achievable. Perhaps the happiest story of them all was the bond that had developed between Cat and Gary and how love had flourished in their new surroundings.

The icing on the cake came with the news that Cat and Gary had decided to get married and wanted the ceremony to take place in the open air in the ruins of the ancient church. The whole island community would be in attendance.

Emma was so pleased for Gary and Cat. She was also coping better with the demands of her pregnancy. Michaela's experience of pregnancy had improved too; the island community was growing.

When the day of the wedding came in early May 2019, it was a focus of celebration for the whole island, one of love, aspiration, creativity and independence. Cat and Gary were able to confirm their commitment to each other in the company of their friends and fellow residents, children and animals.

The island community was secure and set to flourish.

On June 5th 2019, Emma's waters broke at two o'clock in the morning and Cat, Marie-Clare and Farid rushed to be on hand, as consideration of any transfer to hospital had become increasingly unrealistic. The tide would be in, making driving impossible, and any other means of leaving the island too risky. A home birth, it appeared, had become inevitable.

Contingency plans had been made for different eventualities but, in any event, matters progressed too quickly. Farid and Marie-Clare were confident they would not let their own anxieties show about overseeing delivery in such circumstances, trying to reassure Emma as much as possible. Emma had been preparing herself for a hospital birth, if required, but was pleased, if a little anxious, to have the baby at home.

She tried to concentrate on the task in hand, rather than think too much about the risks involved. In the event, Nathan arrived quickly and all concerned were much relieved and delighted with their efforts. Emma had done well, she could feel proud. There was something special about bringing her son into the world in their new home. He would be the first resident born on the island for generations.

Rory brought Poppy in to see her as Bracken bounded in too and the family enjoyed a private moment before Nathan appeared to want feeding and Bracken stood guard as Poppy wondered what new surprises a baby brother might bring. It didn't matter; Nathan was born and was healthy and Emma, if not Rory, was sure that their family was complete.

As the summer progressed, the skies brought a welcome sight. A pair of hawks were seen flying across the island for the first time in many years; it was a good omen.

Ingram Content Group UK Ltd.
Milton Keynes UK
UKHW011836270423
420877UK00004B/408